YOU ARE EXPELLED

Chet Cunningham

Fitzhenry&Whiteside Limited

You Are Expelled

Educational notes and questions by
Arnot McCallum
English Co-ordinator
Windsor Board of Education

Canadian Educational Edition

Cover illustration and design by Kerry Designs

Fitzhenry & Whiteside Limited
195 Allstate Parkway,
Markham, Ontario, L3R 4T8
e-mail: godwit@fitzhenry.ca

Printed and bound in The United States
99 98 97 96 95 / 6 5 4 3 2

ISBN 0-88902-038-8

YOU ARE EXPELLED

Chapter 1

Vinny Walker hunched his shoulders and scowled as he angled his ten-year-old Ford gently toward the curb and eased on the brake.

"Good *Gooney* ... good car," he said, a touch of pride and affection showing as he switched off the lights and killed the engine. He sucked a deep breath and glanced down the street toward Bob's Happy Time Bar. So far, none of the kids had spotted him, but chances were good that his luck couldn't hold. He hated coming down here at night, sneaking around so he wouldn't be seen pulling his old man out of the bar. It was bad enough being heckled by the bar rats inside without the other kids finding out. But the word got around, no matter how careful he was.

The next day at school was pure hell. Some wise guy would make a crack about Vinny's drunken father and that would set it off. That was the trouble with a small town — everyone knew everyone else's business. He could put up with most of the guys, but not Sam White. Sam got hold of the news and everytime gave Vinny a rough go, a damn rough go.

Vinny didn't want even to think about tomorrow. He grabbed the steering wheel and glared through *Gooney's* windshield. His car was the only thing he was proud of; he could depend on *Gooney*, she never let him down. Sure his bucket didn't look so good on the outside, splotched with primer paint, but as soon as he raised the cash he would get a new paint job and some whitewalls.

Vinny knew it was more important to have the mill under the hood in tip top shape than a freshly painted body. He tuned her every week, until *Gooney* purred like a sleek, well-fed cat. He doubted if there were a ten-year-old car in town that ran as well as *Gooney*.

Vinny glanced at his hands. His knuckles around the steering wheel were splotched with whiteness. He let go and pounded a fist on the door. Vinny knew he couldn't stall any more, he had to go inside and drag out his dad. He took a quick look up and down the sidewalk before stepping into the cool night air.

The sign flashed on and off: "BOB'S HAPPY TIME BAR, BOB'S HAPPY TIME BAR." Inert gas, Vinny remembered as he walked quickly toward the sign. Neon, an inert gas in a glass tube excited by an electrical charge .... "Your old man's a drunk!" He pinched his eyes together. For the last month he had averaged two runs a week down here. The bar man was doing them a favor to call. It was either that or bring in the cops. That would mean twenty-five bucks to get the old man out of the drunk tank and Vinny knew his mother couldn't afford it. It was all she could do to keep up with the old man's drinking habit. Bail was impossible. His mom had to support the four of them including Vinny's little brother.

At the door Vinny halted and sucked in another cleansing breath. It was the same kind of quick little gasp he took just before one of his corner jump shots. Only this one was filled with apprehension and fear.

He looked at the familiar sign painted in red letters: "NO ONE PERMITTED UNDER 21, alcoholic beverages served." Glancing down the street toward *Gooney's* battered body, he had a sudden desire to run for the car and burn rubber until he was miles away, forgetting who he was and what he was supposed to do.

Muffled sounds of men's coarse laughter and the lyrics of noisy music blasted out of the bar. Shrugging, Vinny stretched his thin, wiry frame as tall as it would go and pushed the door open.

The scent of sour beer, smoke and popcorn assaulted his nostrils. It was the same sickening mixture that his father reeked of 365 days of the year.

A few heads turned toward him, but the habitues of the bar paid little attention to the blond-haired boy who stood silently in the doorway. He caught Bob's attention and the beefy barman nodded toward the last booth on the far side of the crowded room.

He was halfway across the room when the first heckler's voice called, "Hey, kid, your mama know you're out?"

"Hell, his ma's probably walking the streets herself."

Vinny's face turned red with anger and he tensed his bony arms until they hung stiffly from his sides, his fists clenched. He glanced at the man who had said his mother was walking the streets. It was Al Thompson, a rednecked bull of a man who spent more time looking for a fight than he did drinking beer.

"Bob, you running a Boy's Town here?" another heckler yelled. The bar echoed with laughter as Vinny shuffled toward the dim booth.

The sight made him sick. His father was slumped in a corner booth, his head resting in a pool of spilled beer and cigarette ashes. His clothes were torn and soiled and his face was shadowed with a three-day beard. His father coughed and Vinny turned his head as he saw the vegetable-soup-like fluid gush from his mouth.

"Get that sick drunk outa here," Al yelled. "He stinks worse than a dead pig."

"Come on, Dad," Vinny said, shaking the man's shoulder. No response. Lawrence Walker's head rolled in the viscous liquid and his lips muttered unintelligible words.

"I'll give you a hand, kid." Bob threw a rag over the mess and grunted as he pulled Lawrence Walker to his feet. Vinny watched as the barman dragged his father across the room. When his father started moving his feet Vinny draped one of the drunk man's arms over his shoulder.

"I've got him now, Bob. Thanks," he said.

"Yeah, kid. After you pay me a buck eighty-five."

"How much?"

"Buck eighty-five. A pitcher of beer and two packs of cigarettes." Holding the slobbering man against his hip, Vinny fished out two worn dollar bills and handed them to the barman. Bob returned a dime and nickel and stuffed a bar rag under Lawrence Walker's chin.

"That'll keep him from barfing on himself, kid. Have him bring it back tomorrow." Bob returned to the bar.

Vinny pulled his father along with him as he headed for the door. He hated the limp form he was carrying. He was saving that money to get some new spark plugs. He'd worked all day Sunday for five bucks, giving three of them to his mother. Now, his father had taken the rest. Roughly, Vinny jerked the man along.

"Rolling drunks again, kid?" Al Thompson called. His lips curled back in a sneer as he spoke. He was mean-drunk.

Vinny swallowed hard and turned. He'd taken all he could. It was just like at school when the kids rode him to the limit.

"Shut up! Shut up you dumb jerk!" Vinny cried out, feeling sick and angry. The man's face flushed.

Heads turned. Conversation died. Al slid off his stool, still holding his beeer. His face was expressionless, his eyes cruel. Vinny was sorry as soon as he had spoken. It seemed he was always sorry when it was too late.

"Who you talking to, kid?"

Vinny turned his back, pulling his dad toward the door.

"Who the hell you talking to, boy?" Al roared, stepping between Vinny and the exit.

"Leave me alone, mister."

"Now, that's more respectful, kid," Al grinned, moving toward Vinny. "Just don't forget how to talk to your betters." He turned and winked at the men at the bar whose faces showed various degrees of drunken interest. Behind the bar, Bob looked on with disgust, his big forearms crossed.

As Vinny leaned down to pull his father forward, Al poured the mugful of beer over the struggling pair.

Most of the beer splashed on Vinny. He froze, wanting to smash the man with his fists until he begged him to stop but he knew it wouldn't be that way. Al would pick him up and shake him like a cat shakes a mouse, and with equal pleasure.

While the audience at the bar laughed, Vinny wiped the beer off his face with his sleeve and looked at Al.

"Well, kid, you gonna swing?" Al taunted.

"No," Vinny said. His anger had drained off, leaving him weak and shaky. He dragged his father out into the night.

The cold air partially sobered Larry Walker. He staggered to the car, swinging and flailing his arms, barely able to maintain his balance. Vinny helped him into the back seat where he immediately passed out and began snoring.

As Vinny started for the driver's side, a young policeman walked up and began eyeing *Gooney*.

"Something wrong with my car, Officer?" Vinny asked, sarcastically.

The policeman nodded. "I'd almost bet on it. May I see your driver's licence, please?" The man's eyes narrowed as he surveyed the boy.

Vinny handed him the licence.

"I'd like to see your identification too, Officer."

"You getting smart with me?" The young man's voice revealed his irritation.

"No, sir. I'd just like to see your police I.D. card. I know all the other guys so you must be new." Vinny's voice was guileless, too much so, and he knew he'd pushed his luck too far again when he saw the officer's jaw muscles knot up.

"Don't smart-mouth me, boy! I'm not in the mood. I think you're one of the hot-rodders dragging on Second Street a few minutes ago."

"No, sir, not me. I can prove it. I'd still like to see your police card. I got a right to."

The officer nodded. "Yes, you have. And I got a right to ticket you for every equipment violation I can find on this pile of junk."

The officer sniffed the air, and moved closer.

"You been drinking, boy?"

"No."

"Don't gimme that. You smell like a brewery. Where'd you get the booze?"

"A guy in Bob's Bar pours it on sixteen-year-olds every night."

"Sure, kid. They throw beer all over." His voice was cold, challenging. "Put your hands on top of the car, spread your legs, and lean forward. Don't try anything or I'll split your skull open."

Vinny looked at the nightstick in the cop's hand and cringed. He put his hands on the car. What was going on? Who did this dumb cop think he was, pushing him around like this? He wasn't doing anything wrong!

The officer felt Vinny's pockets, his back, and down each leg. He found nothing.

A city prowl car pulled up, and a gray-haired officer poked his head out the window.

"Trouble, Harry?"

"Got a loud-mouthed kid who smells like a tap room."

"He clean?"

"Yup."

"Good. I know the kid. Let him relax."

"Okay, kid, stand easy."

Vinny pushed away from the car and stood silently.

"You been drinking, Vinny?" the older cop asked.

"No, Dutch, not a drop." Dutch knew him and would believe him. Dutch had known him since Vinny was in diapers.

"You don't smell so good."

"Guy at Bob's poured beer on me, Dutch. Nothing I could do about it."

"You making your usual pickup, Vinny?"

"Yeah, Dutch." He didn't have to be on the defensive with Dutch — he had grown up with Larry Walker.

"I'll vouch for Vinny, Harry. He came to pick up his dad at Bob's place. No danger of Vinny ever touching a drop — Larry drinks enough for ten men."

"I'm gonna check out this pile of scrap iron," Harry said, looking inside the car. "This your old man?"

"Yes sir."

Harry looked at Dutch. Dutch shrugged.

"Happens pretty often, Harry," Dutch said.

Harry pointed at Vinny. “Okay, kid, get inside and turn on the lights, then hit the turn signals.” Vinny watched as the officer checked the front. “Push the dimmer switch. Now, hit the brake.”

The commands came and Vinny complied with each.

“Start the motor and leave it out of gear,” the young cop said. The engine fired on the first crank, and the regulation muffler emitted a quiet, steady purr. “Rev it up,” the cop said.

As Vinny pushed the accelerator, he smiled. There was a heavy drone as the engine raced, but there was nothing excessive about the noise. It was healthy and powerful, and very legal.

Dutch laughed. “Lots of luck, Harry. I spent two hours once checking out this rig in the daylight. Never found as much as a loose nut. You’re wasting your time on this car, Harry. Vinny’s an A-1 mechanic.”

Harry shrugged.

Dutch took Vinny’s license from Harry and handed it to the boy.

“Get out of here, Vinny,” he said. “And don’t forget to work on that jump shot.”

“Thanks, Dutch,” Vinny said, easing away from the curb.

Damn that new cop! He had no cause to try and bust him that way! He hadn’t done a thing wrong. It would be all over school tomorrow. Stopped by the fuzz. Who would be the first smart guy to laugh at him? Sam White, as usual?

The strong, sour stench of beer filled his nostrils. He hated them all — and more than any, he hated the sodden lump in the back seat who was his sad excuse of a father.

Chapter 2

Vinny waded apprehensively through the first two classes the next day at Forestville High before the rumors caught up with him. He had just left English and was walking toward his locker when Randy Spellman, a freshman boy, yelled at him from across the quad.

"Hey, Vinny. Hear you got busted for drunk driving last night. That right?"

"You got it wrong, punk. It was murder one. Now shove off." Vinny tried to act nonchalant but his legs were trembling and his diaphragm tightened so it hurt to breathe.

He turned to his locker and twirled the combination. It didn't open. He kicked the door and tried again. The story had ballooned as it always did. He gritted his teeth and yanked on the lock and it opened.

Drunk driving!

Before he got to world history two more guys asked him about it. He ignored them, shouldering his way past them into the room. His hands were shaking and his face was flushed when he settled down to his seat.

Jim Hawthorne, the best friend he had, winked at him. Jim was short and chunky. He played tennis and chess and was the best carburetor man in school. Vinny liked him because he could talk to him and work with him on cars. And Jim never bugged him.

"Hi, man, how's the wheels?" Jim asked.

"Still turning."

Jim frowned. "Don't blow your cool, man. You look like you're ready to punch somebody."

"You heard?"

"Three versions."

"So?" Vinny challenged, his voice edgy.

"So keep your hands in your pockets, man. That way you *can't* clobber anybody! Forget those guys. Pretend they don't exist."

The teacher rapped his ruler and the class began. Vinny tried to forget, but all through the period he felt the others eyeing him, whispering, spreading the rumors.

Vinny wished there wasn't a noon hour. He was sure somebody would taunt him about his dad. He was glad Jim had the same lunch period. They ran to the parking lot so the could eat their snack lunches in Jim's cut-down Deuce, a 1932 classic Model "B" Ford. Over lunch they talked about how they could make enough money to buy a supercharger for the Deuce. He was glad Jim didn't bring up the business about last night.

On the way back to the main building they passed the senior bench. It was filled with lettermen in their maroon and gold sweaters.

"Hey, Vinny, that new cop in town pretty tough?" someone yelled.

Vinny and Jim angled away from the group, heading for the far door. Before the pair had walked twenty feet, a row of lettermen blocked their path.

"Look, kid, a senior just asked you a question."

Vinny knew who was talking before he looked. Big, dumb Sam White, the two-hundred-and-twenty-pound meatheaded lineman.

"Seniors do lots of stupid things, White," Vinny snarled, his body tensing.

"Bet that's the way you shot off your mouth at that new cop last night when he caught you drinking down at Bob's Bar."

"Shove off, Sam," Jim said stepping in front of the hulking frame. "It's none of your business!"

Vinny felt proud of Jim. He wouldn't last half a round with Sam.

White laughed, paying no attention to Jim. "Don't guess you could get enough to get drunk on at home, Vinny. Not with your old man lapping it up like milk."

Vinny balled his fists and took a step forward. Jim pretended to back out of the way, deliberately falling against Vinny, knocking him aside.

The seniors laughed.

"Damn, Vinny, you're drunk again," Sam snorted, his beefy hands resting on his hips. "Just like your old man, on the juice all day and all night."

Vinny scrambled to his feet. His face burned. He didn't care about size — he'd had enough. His fingernails dug into his palms as he raised his fists.

The five-minute warning bell rung.

"Look at that," Sam said. "Vinny wants to fight during my English class. Miss Hawkins wouldn't like that at all." The lettermen laughed as they moved off toward the main building.

Vinny wanted to run at them like a bull and smash Sam White in the mouth. Instead he slammed his fist into his palm, and cursed bitterly.

Jim pulled his arm. "Come on Vinny, we'll get the big slob next time. We don't want to be late for class."

Vinny tried to clear his mind of everything except his classes the rest of the afternoon. If he let his attention wander for even a second he thought about Sam, and the different ways he was going to get even. Yes, he'd get him all right; he'd get him like he'd never been had before.

Soon his fantasies of revenge claimed all his attention until he was oblivious to all else.

When the last bell rang, he went out the side door and past the bike rack toward the parking lot.

"Hey, Vinny, wait up," Art Scott called.

Vinny stopped and Art ran up to him, his face alight with excitement.

"Is it true come cop found something wrong with your rod? Some equipment violation?"

Vinny's reaction was automatic. All his repressed anger exploded in a straight hard right to Art's face. He felt his knuckles smash against the boy's cheek bone. His left followed through automatically, plowing into Art's stomach.

He realized what he was doing before he hit Art again. The boy jackknifed in agony, hitting the ground on his side, pulling his knees up to his stomach, gasping for air.

"Get up, Art," Vinny said, willing his friend to feel no pain. "I didn't hit you that hard."

Art groaned and looked up, agonized surprise still on his face.

Vinny looked around, saw no one, and ran to the parking lot. He started *Gooney* and roared from the lot, laying twin belts of burned rubber on the pavement. Miss Hawkins hurried out and bent over Art Scott's crumpled figure. She had watched the whole incident from her window.

At eight-thirty that evening, Mr. Johnson, vice-principal at Forestville High, entered the Blue Flame restaurant and cocktail lounge a half mile out of town on Highway 78. He asked the cashier which waitress was Mrs. Walker.

Gloria Walker stood beside the back booth as the tall, gaunt man told her the story. She looked older than her forty-one years. Her hair was bleached, tinted and set, but her face was puffy and wrinkled. She nervously rubbed her right wrist as she listened to Mr. Johnson tell her about Vinny's unprovoked attack on Art Scott. He told her that Vinny had a good record up to this time and the administration had taken that into consideration.

"Mrs. Walker, the principal has made the decision and I'm only delivering it to you." He took out a letter and handed it to her. She read it slowly, tears welling in her hazel eyes.

Due to an unprovoked attack upon Art Scott, your son, Vincent Walker, is hereby suspended for a period of five school days beginning tomorrow. Before readmission he must apologize to Art Scott and attend a conference with Mr. Johnson, vice-principal.

Gloria Walker gazed past the vice-principal's shoulder. There was a long silence. "I try, Mr. Johnson. Vinny's my oldest. He's a good boy. Don't know why he'd hurt that other kid, but I'll have a talk with him tomorrow." She stuffed the letter in her skirt pocket and rubbed her eyes with the back of her hand.

She stood there, staring at the wall, as the man nodded and started to walk away.

Mr. Johnson felt the need to say something reassuring. "I hope for Vinny's sake this doesn't happen again," he said.

Mrs. Walker watched as he turned and left. She went to the restroom, read the letter again and cried.

When Vinny woke up the next morning, his right hand was swollen and throbbing. As he ran hot water on it he was sorry he had hit Art. He didn't mean Art any harm. He just happened to be there instead of Sam White. The trouble was, he'd been holding back all his life. People kept putting him down. *Don't do this, don't do that. Wait until you're older.* He was getting fed up with everyone telling him what to do! He was sick of being pushed around.

He knew hitting Art would cost him, but he didn't know what. When would the axe fall? After school today?

He looked at the battered alarm clock on his dresser. Nine-thirty! It couldn't be. He was late for school! He started to dress. When he reached for his car keys he saw a letter and a note.

Vinny. You can't go to school today. Read the letter. I shut off your alarm last night. Please stay home until I get up about eleven o'clock. We'll have a talk.

Vinny doubled his fist and chopped at the air after he read the letter.

He read it again and pulled on a pair of old pants and a T-shirt. Five days! He had heard about a kid who had a five-day for hot-rodding around the school parking lot. Five days! He thought about the make-up work he'd have when he went back.

He saw that his younger brother, Hal, had gone to school. His mom must have got up and sent him off, then gone back to bed. She had to sleep in late, since she didn't get home from work until three a.m.

Vinny moped around. He had toast, jam and milk for breakfast, then watched an old movie on TV, then turned off the tube and wandered outside. *Five* days! What would he do? Get a job and earn some loot? Where? *What could he do? Get a job raking leaves?* He didn't like the idea of work while he still had a few bucks. He thought about what Dutch Van Dyke had said about working on his corner jump shot. *Why not? He had to get in shape for basketball season anyway.*

He backed *Gooney* out of the drive and parked it, then rolled his mother's car down the slope and put it at the curb.

The regulation hoop with a chain net had been mounted on the front of the garage for two years. Vinny sometimes practiced for hours on his lay-up, on a hook and corner jump shot. He'd played on the JV squad last year as a sophomore and the coach had encouraged him to keep up practice.

The ball felt good in his hands. He pulled off his shoes and took a shot. Swish. He got the ball, dribbled, turned and hooked. The ball spun around the rim, teetered and fell away. He repeated the swift, graceful pattern twenty times, sinking the last three in a row.

When he took a break for a glass of milk, he smelled smoke and ran into the living room. He found his father sleeping on the sofa. Beside his limp figure smoke billowed up from one of the foam cushions.

Vinny grabbed the smouldering cushion and ran to the back yard, where he doused it with water. He shook it out and a soggy cigarette butt fell off the damp cushion.

In the living room Vinny found the pack of cigarettes and matches scattered on the floor. *He's gonna kill us all before he's through*, Vinny thought. They were the same words his mother used before his dad lost his driver's license. Vinny looked at his father and shook his head in disgust. The man had not moved. He lay there snoring, the sour smell of beer mingling with the odor of burned upholstery.

Okay, Vinny, let's move it, he said to himself. *Do something before you blow your cool!*

He went back to the hoop and shot baskets until his arms ached. After putting the ball away, he started running around the block. He sprinted for twenty yards, then trotted. Alternating between the two speeds, Vinny headed around the block, breathing deeply, but soon gasping for air.

When he had circled the block twice, he went in for a shower. As the hot water poured over him, he remembered his mom's note about having a talk. She probably wouldn't get around to it. She never did. She had too many other things on her mind. Vinny knew this five-day suspension could set him back in school. Slugging Art was *his* stupid play of the week. Lately, everything seemed to be going wrong. He always got he dirty end of the stick. But things would change, he vowed. Things would change.

For the rest of his suspension, Vinny worked at shooting baskets and running. Every morning and every afternoon he put in at least three hours. He was his own boss and nobody put him down, nobody gave him a raw deal.

Chapter 3

Vinny went back to classes Wednesday. He wheeled into the student parking lot and spotted Jim polishing the hood of his Deuce. Vinny parked *Gooney* beside the venerable Deuce.

"How're the wheels?" Vinny called, revving up *Gooney* before he put her fire out.

"Going round and round, man," Jim said. "Great to have you back, Vin. It's been dull around here."

"Yeah, I bet Sam hasn't had anybody to ride all week."

"Haven't heard much from him." Jim brushed a smudge off the Deuce's hood.

"Probably saving all his firepower for me," Vinny said. They walked on to the quad and Vinny waved to Jim as he turned in at the vice-principal's office. Art Scott was already there. He eyed Vinny solemnly, then grinned and held out his hand.

"Jim told me how Sam bugged you that day, Vinny. Sorry I mouthed off."

Vinny gripped Art's extended hand. He felt ashamed that Art was apologizing to *him*.

"Thanks, Art. Sorry I hit you. Lost my head I guess." Vinny looked down, unable to meet Art's frank, friendly gaze.

"Forget it, maybe we can both clobber Sam one of these days." Art said. Vinny looked up at the boy and smiled.

"Thanks Art. Thanks a lot."

Mr. Johnson motioned Vinny into his office. He settled back in his chair and stared at Vinny, who stood uncomfortably before him.

"Vincent, your five-day suspension is over. I hope it has taught you something. Violence is never the answer to any problem. Did you apologize to Art?" His voice was firm. He was a no-nonsense man.

Vinny nodded.

"Good, now keep your hands to yourself and you should get along fine the rest of the year. Any questions?"

"No sir." Vinny glared at the man. Why hadn't he asked him about the fight? He stood convicted without a trial, like the young cop had treated him.

"You're excused, Vincent."

He hurried out to try to get to his first class on time, seething with anger. When would someone hear his side of the story?

He barely made it to his math class before the last bell, and nobody had time to razz him about his suspension. A few of the kids looked at him in surprise, and whispered to their neighbors, but no one spoke directly to him.

He got makeup assignments after each period. Five days of work, and each teacher piled it on. He felt loaded down when he and Jim left world history for lunch. They found a spot under the twisted maples on the south lawn, sprawled in the shade and began eating.

They didn't talk much. Vinny drifted into his fantasy world where no one knew about his dad, nor where his mother worked. In his dream world everyone had to judge him by what he was, and what he did. He was a straight-A student. Everyone knew his name and spoke to him pleasantly. He had made his letter his sophomore year on the varsity hoop squad and now he was going to be team captain!

A swishing of brown skirt erased Vinny's illusion. He saw two long, slender legs curl up under the skirt as a girl sat down in front of Jim.

"Hi, Jim," she said sweetly. "Can you give me a lift home tonight? I promised not to ask unless it was dreadfully important, but I've got just stacks and stacks of books, and ... I mean, would it be okay?"

Jim turned to her and groaned. "Come on, Kathy, knock it off and bug out. You said you wouldn't bother me this year, right? Now get lost!" Jim turned to Vinny. "How about this bird, trying to bum a ride home in *my* Deuce!"

"Yeah," Vinny said absently. "Tough."

"Please, Jim," she pleaded. Jim looked at Vinny as if she weren't there. "Last summer you wanted me to help you polish the Deuce, and you said you'd give me lots of rides home, remember?"

"Kathy, you're just a sophomore, now shove off and get lost. I can't waste my time on you. I dig senior chicks."

Kathy squeezed between Jim and Vinny, bumping into both in the process. She looked at Vinny.

"Talk, talk, Jim Hawthorne, that's all you do. Why I know for a fact that you haven't had one single date this year."

Kathy looked questioningly at Vinny. He was back in his beautiful, fantasy world. His eyes were glazed as he imagined himself being lifted on his teammates' shoulders for making the game-winning basket of the year.

"Vinny, what do you think of that? This super crumb leads me on about rides, and now he chickens out when I've got this stack of books to get home."

Vinny forced himself back to reality. He thought someone had said something to him.

"You with us, Vinny? Are you tripping out? Vinny? You've got a creep here for a friend."

Vinny shook his head. It was Kathy Bell, "Little Kathy," they had called her two summers ago. She was no longer little. She lived across the street from Jim and had been a monumental nuisance when the two had rebuilt the Deuce that summer.

"Vinny, you going out for basketball this year?" she asked, chattily, her brown eyes wide, her teeth gleaming in the sunlight.

Jim groaned. "Oh, no! Football season isn't over and she starts lining up her basketball boyfriend. You should get a letter for your team spirit, Kathy."

She ignored Jim.

"Yeah, I guess. Sure I'm going out for the team. Why?"

"She's making a team survey to pick the most promising victim," Jim said. He ducked as Kathy swung her purse at him.

Vinny grinned. Kathy had done a lot of filling out in two years. How come he hadn't noticed?

"Why you asking if I'm turning out?" Vinny asked, leaning on his elbow and chewing a blade of grass.

She smiled, her brown eyes dancing. "That's a terrible thing to ask a girl, Vinny. Especially when a girl isn't supposed to let a boy know that she likes him and thinks he's good looking." She fluttered her lashes and Jim groaned, putting his hands to his temples.

"Then don't tell me," he said standing up. She popped up like a jack-in-the-box beside him. Her height surprised him, she was so tall, probably five-feet-seven.

"I'm still looking for a hand with my books, tonight. Vinny, could you help me? Jim's too stingy to give me a lift."

"Aw, Kathy, knock it off," Jim said disgustedly, still holding his head as if in pain.

Vinny laughed. "You never were bashful, were you? Remember when we used to call you bankrupt, because you were so flat-busted?"

Kathy giggled. "Hey, that was a thousand years ago when I was a little kid. What about it, Vinny?" she said. "Be a sport, live dangerously and take me home?"

"Kathy, won't you learn?" Jim wailed. "Girls just don't ask a guy to take them home! Look out, Vinny, she's trying to hook you."

Vinny grinned at Kathy, paying no attention to Jim. "Sure, I'll take you home." She gave him her locker number and walked toward the science building.

"You flipped, big buddy? That's just skinny old Kathy, remember? She lives across the street from me and she's nothing but arms and legs."

Vinny shook his head. "If you think she's still just arms and legs, Jim, you need glasses."

They moved toward the door.

"Well, look there, Vinny's back," someone said.

It was Sam and three of his football buddies.

"Drop dead, White," Vinny said. The four stood on the edge of the steps, making the other kids squeeze past them to get in the door. Vinny and Jim moved forward.

"How does it feel, kid, getting suspended?" Sam asked, grinning, gloating.

"Think you'd come back a big hero?" Sam's lieutenant, Billy Jansen chirped.

"Drop dead, Sam," Vinny said as he moved toward the door. Sam's hand reached out to grab Vinny's shirt. Vinny saw it coming and chopped his fist down. His knuckles slammed across Sam's wrist. The boy cried out in pain.

Vinny and Jim pushed past the group, propelled by the students behind them. Vinny glanced over his shoulder and saw Sam rubbing his wrist. Vinny felt good.

The only other person to mention his suspension that day was his English teacher when she gave him the make-up work. She said she was glad he was back.

After his last class, Vinny found Kathy's locker and leaned back to wait. He noticed she was more than just tall and slender as she swung down the hall toward him.

"Vinny! Hi," she called when she saw him. "You really came!"

Vinny felt like running. He had never taken a girl home from school before.

"Been waiting long?"

He shook his head and reached for her books, piling them on top of his own.

"I've got a little make-up work tonight," he explained.

"I know." Her eyes met his. It was a strange new feeling. They were talking without saying words. Her eyes were saying, "I think you're cute, Vinny."

They walked to the school entrance before he stopped.

"Hey, almost forgot old *Gooney*, my wheels," he said. "She's out in the lot."

"Oh, no," Kathy said. Vinny, I can't ride in your car. My mother ...."

"Say no more, if you walk, I walk."

"Let me fill you in about the Ancients," Kathy said. "They say I have to have any car checked out by them before I can ride in it. Big deal. Jim's car got the okay, so yours should too, that is, if you want me to ride some time?"

Vinny kicked an empty paper sack on the sidewalk.

"Sure. Why wouldn't I want you to ride? Parents are the hang-up. They put us down every chance they get! Making you get a safety inspection before you can ride in a guy's car." *It's me they'll really inspect*, he thought.

"Creepy," Kathy agreed, "But I have to do it."

"Did you ever try to talk with your folks, you know, about important stuff like what you want to be when you grow up?" he asked, trying to change the subject. As soon as her folks heard the name Walker, *Gooney* would flunk out.

"Yeah," Kathy said, catching one of the books that was slipping. "They get hung-up on those prehistoric ideas. Like me being a nurse, or a teacher. You know, Vinny?"

Vinny shifted the books to his other hip as they crossed the street. No, he didn't know. His parents never bothered talking to him. They didn't care, one way or the other.

"One guy I really can talk to is Joe Carney, down at the Shell station. I mean, he loans me tools and all that jazz. But most Ancients won't even try to listen."

"Maybe we should set up an audio-audio club," she said, skipping beside him. "We meet in this big room and the kids talk and the parents listen. It would be groovy. Everyone saying things, sorta."

"You're nuts!" he said, laughing. He shook his head. "That would be a change, though. My mom won't listen. When I try to talk to her she's either too tired, or too busy, or we can't afford it, or she's gonna take time out in just a minute. That minute never comes."

They went down another block and were at her house.

"Come in for a Coke and listen to some records, Vinny."

"No, I've got hours of homework to do. By the time I get dinner and all ...." He handed her the books.

"Sure you can't come in for just a half a minute?" Their eyes met and he felt like he had a mouthful of cotton.

He shook his head. "Lunch tomorrow at the maples?" he finally asked, his ears burning with embarassment.

She nodded. He turned and jogged back the way he had come. *Maybe, just maybe, things will be different*, he thought. As he ran he began to fantasize again. He was the star letterman, people were cheering him, and Kathy was there — his girl Kathy.

Chapter 4

"Vinny?" his mother called from the kitchen.

"Yeah?"

"When your mother calls you, boy, get off your ass and go see what she wants!" his dad yelled.

When he wasn't drunk his dad was loud-mouth mean, Vinny thought. He pushed up from the floor and walked around his brother, Hal, and into the kitchen, his hands jammed into his pockets.

"Yeah, Mom?"

"Sit down, Vinny, I thought we could talk a minute while I finish breakfast."

Vinny sat. Mrs. Walker wore a robe, hadn't combed her hair yet, and there were traces of last night's makeup still around her eyes. In the harsh morning light Vinny realized how old his mother looked.

Another Saturday session. He was getting to hate Saturday mornings. He knew what it would be — the quiz about school-work, the lecture about good grades and graduating, and worst of all, the guilty tears and eventual argument.

"How's the school work coming, Vinny?"

"Fine."

"Well, how much of it you got done?"

"Half."

"Are you going to finish today?"

"No."

"Oh, Vinny! You know what I'm asking. Why not just tell me all about it, instead of making me ask you a thousand questions?"

"Okay, I'm sorry!" He sighed, and began to rattle off the list which was now beginning to sound like a broken record. "I got all my math and history done. I'll finish English this afternoon. Tomorrow I'll do my physics for science and I didn't have anything for gym or shop."

She put down a sweet roll and reached for his hand.

"Vinny, I know you had a rough week, but you came through it fine." She patted his hand as she spoke. "I got my hopes pinned on you, Vinny. In another year and a half you'll be out of high school. You got to finish school so's you can get a good job. Your pa never had no chance, him just finishing the seventh grade, and me just one year of high school. Vinny, I got to see you don't wind up like your pa."

"We been over this a thousand times...." Vinny said.

She waved her hand, stopping him. "Vinny, I know there's lots of things other kids your age have, you don't, but I'll make it up to you. I know how it feels, Vinny. I was your age once."

"Sure, Mom," Vinny's tone was bored.

She looked at him angrily. "I don't like the way you say that. Just remember who pays the damned bills around here! When I was your age I was out on my own." Her anger fled as quickly as it rose. "But I don't want you to do that," she said, dabbing at her eyes, "Why do you think I try to keep us together? Sure I could get the government to pay us."

"Okay, Mom. I'm sorry I said that. Just don't cry."

"What the hell's the trouble?" Larry Walker growled, coming up behind Vinny's chair. No one answered.

"What the hell's going on, I asked? What's the trouble?"

"You're the trouble," Vinny muttered.

"What was that, kid? You sassing me?"

"I said, *you are the trouble!* The town drunk! The big joker, but no one laughs at you. They laugh at me, and Mom and Hal."

"It's time I gave you another whipping, boy. You're getting too big for your britches."

"You couldn't whip me last time you tried. You can't now." Vinny yelled at him.

"You make your mother cry again, kid, and I'll show you I can whip you. You're getting too big to use my belt on — I'll use my fists." His anger seemed to sober Larry Walker.

"Sure you will." Vinny said, starting for the door. His father stepped in the way but Vinny pretended he was dribbling and made a fake one way and darted the other when his father stumbled the wrong way.

He ran for the sidewalk, sprinting hard, elbows pumping, blasting all-out. After a block he slowed to a walk panting for air, then jogged for a while before sprinting again.

Damn him, Vinny thought. Why didn't his old man go on a five-year drunk and stop bothering them? There never was enough money, but he always got his bottle! Maybe if he were gone his mom wouldn't have it so tough. I would certainly make it easier for Vinny, with no more calls from Bob's Bar to come and haul out the body.

Vinny ran hard again, arms pumping, legs churning. On the back side of the big block he jogged, resting.

"*Don't end up like your father,*" his mom was always throwing up to him. He got so tired of hearing it he wanted to take *Gooney* and head out some place and never come back!

If he could only get a job and move out. But it would be a year and a half more before he could get a full-time job. One kid he knew quit school last year and went to work, though. He was earning a hundred and sixty-five a week!

"But I don't want to quit," Vinny said aloud. He liked school, except for guys like Sam White, and now basketball season was coming up it would really be good if he made the cut and got to stay on the varsity squad this year. That would be great!

No one was outside when he circled back to his house. He slid into *Gooney* and fired her up. He took off down the street, having remembered that Jim was going to give his Deuce a tuneup today.

When he got to Jim's place he looked across the street wondering if Kathy was home. The wings of the Deuce's hood were both up, and Jim's head was hidden by them.

"'Bout time you got here, big buddy," Jim called. "I'm having fits with my timing. Must have put the new points in wrong."

Vinny looked at the distributor and saw the problem. He made a few adjustments and the Deuce started, then they drove to Joe's Shell Station at the other end of town to use a timing light.

Joe Carney, who was about Jim's size, liked to soup-up hot rods and had a dragster of his own. He let the boys use tools and sometimes helped them when business was slow, so kids came from all over town to get gas at his station.

"I probably lose money on the kids," he told his wife. "But I remember when I was that age with my first car and no money."

"Hi, Joe, how's it go?" Jim called. He bought a dollar's worth of gas, then told Joe his problem.

"Wheel her in the stall, Jim. You know where the timing light is. Can't stand to hear a Deuce sputtering that way."

It took them five minutes to set the timing. Jim put the tools back where they belonged, and thanked Joe.

"How's *Gooney* running, Vin? Haven't seen you and your Ford for a while."

"Runs great, just got no loot for the old petrol," Vinny said apologetically

They waved and drove out of the station. The rig had to be road tested, so Jim swung the Deuce out of town on a gravel road and up a long hill. He nodded appreciatively at the sound of the engine.

"She runs good, Vin. Should be okay for another five thousand miles. By then she'll need a major tune and we'll tear her down, carb and all."

A half hour later when they returned, Kathy was raking leaves.

"Hi, Vinny," she called.

"Watch out for that man-trap," Jim warned.

Vinny ran across the street. "Hi, doll."

"Well, hey, how's it going?"

"Need some help with the leaves?"

"Heck, no! I was just faking it until you came back. How goes the battle with your folks?"

"Lousy. Why do parents have to be such creeps?"

"You got me. What happened?"

"Nothing much. Just a battle. I can't even remember what it started about. Dad came in sore about something and lit the fuse. Bam!"

He took the rake and pulled some leaves into the pile.

"How about listening to some records? We'll have some cookies or something and I'll figure out a way to get Mom to check *Gooney.*"

"Into the valley of death, huh?"

"Chin up!" she said, leading him inside. Mrs. Bell was in the kitchen.

"Mom, this is Vinny Walker. Vinny, my mom."

"How do you do," Vinny stammered, not knowing whether to offer to shake hands or what.

She looked at him coolly. She was tall and lean, reminding Vinny of a tough hickory sapling.

"Vinny Walker. Yes, I've heard about you. Katherine talks about you a lot." She turned to the girl. "I've got a lot to do, Katherine, if you'll excuse me."

"Mom! I told you I wanted you to look at Vinny's car. Can't you take time now to walk outside for a few minutes?"

"Katherine, I don't appreciate your talking in that tone of voice," her mother said. But she turned to the front door. "Let's take a look, though," she said.

Mrs. Bell didn't like *Gooney* at all.

"Do you have a safety inspection sticker on your car?" she asked.

"No Ma'am, but it would pass, easy."

"Easily is correct."

"Yes, Ma'am."

"Have you good brakes?"

"Yes."

"Ever had an accident?"

"Mother!"

"I'm only thinking of you, Katherine." She turned back to Vinny. "Ever had a wreck?"

"No."

"Well, the car is old, and my husband says old cars have more accidents. He'll have to give final approval." She turned abruptly and walked back into the house.

Kathy sputtered. She glared at her mother's back as she went into the house.

"Oh, sometimes she makes me so mad! She didn't give you or *Gooney* a chance!"

"We're the only Walker family in town. She tuned-out as soon as she heard my name."

"I'll talk to her."

"Sure, Kathy."

"See you Monday?"

"Lunch?" he asked.

"Great. And don't worry. I'll work it out."

"Sure, Kathy." He crawled into *Gooney* and fired the mill. He looked back as he gunned away, waving. He knew it would be a long time before Mrs. Bell gave her approval for Kathy to ride in his car. She didn't like him. The rhyme "To hell, with Mrs. Bell," kept running through his mind. He forced a grin, but it didn't make him feel any better.

Chapter 5

Monday morning Vinny's alarm woke him at 7:30. He got up and roused his brother.

"Come on, Hal, time to get up. Come on, roll out. How about some hotcakes for breakfast?"

"Hey, yeah man! Can I help pour 'em?"

"Sure, squirt, just get dressed."

A few minutes later, while Vinny was combing his hair in the bathroom, Hal edged in front of him. Hal tried to comb his hair exactly the way his big brother did.

"Vinny, could we go down to Merry Brook after school and shoot the BB gun at tin cans like we used to?"

"We'll see, kid. Might be fun at that. I got a sort of thing planned with Jim, but I'll see." He suddenly realized his dad had talked to him like that when he was ten.

As Hal poured the second round of batter on the griddle, Vinny went to check his dad. He never ate breakfast, but Vinny always checked just out of habit.

He wasn't in his room, and the bed hadn't been slept in.

"Great!" Vinny said. He phoned City Hall. After listening to what the desk sergeant said, Vinny cradled the phone in disgust. This time it was drunk and disorderly, resisting arrest and panhandling, bail one big one. If Larry pleaded guilty he'd get thirty days or a two hundred dollar fine.

It had happened before. His dad would plead guilty and take the thirty days. At least that would keep him sober for a month, Vinny thought. Maybe he'd try to get a job when he came out this time.

Vinny left his mom a note telling about his dad. He didn't want to got to school. It would be another rough day. He thought of splitting, maybe driving up on some hill, just watching the world go by. It would be fun if Kathy would come with him. Fat chance! She was too sensible to do such a dumb thing. "Why ask for more trouble by ditching classes?" she'd ask.

He drove Hal to his school on the way to Forestville High. He timed it so he slid into his first class seat just before the tardy bell. He spent most of the time between periods in the boy's room. He wasn't going to give anyone, least of all Sam, the chance to razz him. After today it would be forgotten.

He was lucky. Somehow, the word hadn't gotten out, or maybe punching Art had served some useful purpose after all. He saw Kathy and they decided to walk home through the park. When the last bell rang, he threw his books into his locker and hurried over to Kathy.

"Hi, doll." He forced his voice to be light.

"Hi, Vinny. I got a new record at home you've just got to hear! It's by this new group, the Groovy Gumbos."

Vinny laughed at the name. They talked about school and the football team, and a clique of seniors that had all the student government offices tied up. They headed through the park two blocks from school where a big house had once stood in a grove of oak and pine trees. The block had been given to the city as a park, but little had been done to develop it. There were some swings, and an open area for games, and under the trees, some picnic tables.

"Did you hear about my dad?" Vinny asked her.

She shook her head.

"He got picked up last night drunk and caused some trouble so he's in jail for thirty days." Vinny felt compelled to tell her. He had never volunteered bad news of the family to anyone before, but Kathy listened to him. He guessed that made the difference.

"Gee, that's too bad, Vinny." Her face clouded for a moment, then a smile washed away the frown. "Hey, I've got a chance to work out with the yell squad! How about that? Wouldn't it be terrific if I made the yell squad and you made the varsity? We could go to all the games together. The other girls would flip!"

Vinny felt sort of let down. He'd expected a different reaction from her when she heard about his dad. He didn't know exactly what, but not this. Didn't she *care* if his old man was a drunk?

They were angling across the park toward the tall swings.

"Come on, don't be an old man grump! Have some fun, kick up your heels a little. It's time to live, man! Hey, send me on a cheap trip on the swing. Okay? Really swing me high!"

Vinny relaxed. *I'm up-tight again. Kathy's right*, he thought. *It's not important to other people.* He pushed the swing and sent her sailing into space.

Still it bugged him. "Kathy, you think I should just laugh it off when the kids tease me about my dad?" he asked.

"Golly, no, Vinny. Just ignore them. If you play it cool they'll leave you alone soon."

"Ignore Sam?" That was a laugh. He pushed her hard, running under the swing, giving it an extra boost. When he walked back from the big push he saw four guys sitting on the picnic table nearby.

"Looky, there's old Vinny," Sam White said. "Town drunk's kid really moving up in society. Look who he's walking home!"

Beside Sam on the table were Bull Knapp and Johnny Sinclair and another kid Vinny didn't know.

Kathy let the swing die while she looked on, quietly, then she got out of the swing and pulled on Vinny's arm.

"Let's ignore these freaks and leave," she said.

As they turned to leave three of the boys blocked their path.

"Kathy, what's a nice girl like you doing with a rat like Vinny?"

The new kid said it. Vinny wondered who he was and how well Kathy knew him.

He moved out in front of the others.

"Hey, Vinny," he said, "I hear you're tough. All you have to do is walk through me and you can walk on home with Kathy."

"Don't pay Lars any attention, Vinny," she said. "Just take me home."

They turned aside but Sam blocked them. They were boxed in.

Vinny handed his sweater to Kathy.

"Which one, Sam?" he asked. "Never heard of you doing your own fighting."

"I'm too big for you, Vinny. I'd murder you and you ain't worth it. I save my light work for Lars." Sam waved at the new boy, who pulled off his shirt and threw it to the ground.

"Kathy leaves first," Vinny demanded.

"She stays," Sam said. "You think I want her going for the cops?"

"She goes, Sam. I can outrun any of you jerks. She goes or I take off and you'll never catch me. If any of you weirdos touch her I'll yell cop so loud the whole town will know."

Sam shrugged.

Vinny touched Kathy's elbow. "Get out of here fast, and don't come back!"

There was no fear in her eyes, only anger. "Sam White, you're an animal, you know that? A big, ugly, animal!" She turned and ran toward the street.

Vinny looked at the new kid. He was an inch or so shorter than Vinny, but his chest and arms looked like a weight lifter's. Vinny squared off, trying to remember all he'd ever learned about fighting.

They circled, testing each other, both wary. Vinny drove in his left, flicking it against Lars' jaw. Lars' left came up but his right covered his mid-section.

Vinny blocked a left, then caught a hard right over his heart. It staggered him, but Lars didn't follow his advantage.

Vinny stopped sparring. He wasn't a good boxer. His only hope was to wade in and swarm all over Lars.

It worked the first time. He smashed down Lars' defense and pounded him five or six times about the head and stomach before Lars got away.

The new kid was more careful after that, moving, weaving, bobbing. Lars had fought a lot, Vinny could tell.

Lars worked methodically. After the first few minutes, Vinny's arms felt as if they were weighted. He could hardly hold them up. There were no three-minute rounds here. Lars began getting to Vinny's face and stomach.

When he ducked, Lars was ready with a right that smashed into Vinny's chin like a bomb, lifting him to his toes. He rammed his left into Vinny's unprotected stomach and then a solid right to the nose that knocked Vinny to the dirt.

Vinny shook his head, slowly. He breathed heavily for a moment then got to his knees, then slowly to his feet.

Lars came at him and Vinny swung a wild one that caught Lars on the bridge of the nose, breaking the skin, and blood oozed down his cheek.

His own left hand jabbed Vinny's nose three times so fast it felt like one jarring blow. Vinny felt like a giant punching bag.

Unable to feel pain any longer, or to defend himself, Vinny sank to his knees, too tired to move. Someone planted a foot in his back and pushed him on his face.

"Next time, Vinny," said Sam White, "don't get smart with me. I always pay back my debts."

Vinny heard them laughing, then everything faded out.

Chapter 6

Vinny felt the coldness first. Nothing else registered, just cold. Soon it was cold and wet. As he struggled back to full consciousness he was aware of pain everywhere. He blinked and his vision cleared somewhat.

The blurred face that bent over him seemed far away, a pretty, longish face with brown hair falling around it.

"Vinny? Come on, Vinny, wake up. Wake up, Vinny, come on."

He tried to reply but a cloth covering his mouth garbled it. He blinked again to get his eyes into focus and saw Kathy bending over him. His head was in her lap. He brought his hand up to move the cloth and she caught it.

"Oh, Vinny, I was just about to go for help. I thought you'd never come to. I was afraid your neck was broken."

She took the wet cloth off his face and dabbed it at his forehead and cheeks. His nose throbbed, and his mouth felt cut up inside.

"How long was I out?" he asked.

"Several minutes. I was hiding behind the hedge. I thought you had him for a while."

"You're a ding-a-ling, Kathy."

"That's what people are always telling me," she said, using the scarf to clean his forehead.

He sat up. His stomach felt pulverized and his head pounded, but he made it with Kathy steadying him.

"Kathy," he mumbled through battered lips, "don't tell anybody about this."

"I think you ought to go to the police, Vinny. If you'd whipped Lars you'd have to fight the next one till you got beat."

"No!" he said emphatically. "Besides, I'm gonna get even with Sam, so I don't want this blabbed around."

"Sam and you would be a mismatch. He's twice as heavy as you."

"It's something I gotta do though. Sam's got it coming. Nobody razzed me about my dad until this year when Sam started it. Right now I'd like to kill him!"

"Right now you better get home and get patched up if you aren't going to the police. Give me the keys to *Gooney* and I'll drive her over here to pick you up."

"You don't have a license."

"So what? You can't walk to the lot."

He stood up, swaying dizzily for a moment.

"Who can't? Look at me! Now get out of here and go home. Your mom will have the bloodhounds out looking for you if you're gone much longer."

He took a step away from her, but one knee gave way and he almost fell. She caught him, swinging his arm around her shoulder, pulling his wrist down hard to brace him. With her assistance, he concentrated on keeping his feet moving forward. At the edge of the park, Kathy kissed his cheek.

"You're doing just great! But are you going to make me lug you all the way?"

He loosened his arm and she let it drop from her shoulder and he found he could make his way. She held his arm with both hands anyway as they circled behind the school to the parking lot.

Vinny was worn out by the time he slumped into the driver's seat of the Ford. He tried to find a comfortable place on the seat but there wasn't any.

"Drop me off a block from home," Kathy said as she slid in beside him. "Mom will never know."

Vinny had no trouble driving, except that it hurt to turn his head at the intersections. He took it slow, being careful not to go past Kathy's house.

At the corner she got out, then leaned in the window. "Vinny, you'll feel lots better tomorrow."

He reached across the seat toward her. "Thanks, Kathy, for the help. You're not half the scatterbrain you try to make people think you are."

She waved and ran down the street.

Vinny drove across town carefully, glad when he parked in front of home. He had to admit he felt better, although he knew he'd have sore ribs for a few days, and his nose would probably have a new bend.

It was four o'clock. He wanted to lie down and take a nap, but he knew he'd never get up in time to make dinner, so he set out the food for the evening meal. Hal came in looking worried.

"Hey, Vinny, I busted my sling shot. Can you fix it?"

Vinny took it and tied the strip of inner tube around the leather pocket.

"That should do it, buddy."

"How about shooting at tin cans?"

"Not today, Hal."

Hal looked closer at Vinny's face and frowned.

"Who clobbered you?"

"Well, there was this guy who was ten feet tall, see? He had a big club and he sneaked up behind me ...."

"Aw, you're fooling."

"Yeah."

"Where's Dad?"

"He's in jail, Hal. Be there about a month."

"Darn, he was teaching me how to play checkers."

"Tell you what, Hal. You help me with the dishes and I'll have a game with you, okay?"

Hal nodded and began clearing the table.

Every time Vinny moved a new ache cropped up. It reminded him of Sam and a plan of attack began to form. He could get back at Sam without it costing him a thing. Best of all, the danger factor was low, so no one would know who was doing it!

He worked out the details as he rinsed his mouth with hot salt water, then he took a long shower and felt better. Just knowing he had a plan for Sam kindled a small flame of warmth in him.

After dinner, Vinny turned on TV until Hal finished his homework, then they had two checker games. At eight-thirty he shooed Hal to bed.

In his own room, he slipped into black pants and dark T-shirt. He pocketed a handful of wooden matches and after checking on Hal to be sure he was asleep, he borrowed his brother's bike and pedaled through back streets to Seventh Avenue, where Sam White lived.

He rode past the house, staying on the far sidewalk. Everything was quiet. The garage door was closed and the porch light off. Vinny left the bike across the street and slipped through the shadows to Sam's Camaro in the driveway. Unscrewing the front valve cap, he jammed a match down against the inside of the valve, pressing the plunger down and letting the air hiss out. The matchstick wedged in solidly, holding the valve open. He moved to the other front wheel. Soon all four tires were going flat and Vinny mounted the bike. He laughed all the way home.

The next morning when he met Jim in the parking lot the little guy whistled.

"Hey, buddy, you must have been in a real brawl last night."

Vinny told him about the fight. He had two Band-aids on his chin, and one above his eye. Two or three other bruises blotched his face, but neither eye was black.

By noon several guys had asked him what happened, but he put them off with wisecracks. When he found that Sam had been late to school, he was elated.

Vinny and Jim ate lunch in the Deuce. He felt uneasy about *Gooney*. As dumb as Sam was he'd know who'd done him in and he'd be gunning to do the same thing to *Gooney*. After lunch Vinny searched for Kathy to explain why he hadn't eaten with her at the maples.

As soon as she saw him she gasped.

"Wow! Vinny, you're all bruises!"

"Tell me something new."

She laughed. "Your face looks like a truck ran over it. How do you feel?"

He said he hurt all over.

"You should find out how the winner feels. He can't be in very good shape either." She brushed her hair back from her face. "Vinny, was it you who let the air out of Sam's tires?"

"Who gave you that idea?"

"Come on, man. Sam won't need proof. He knows you did it."

"Maybe I *want* him to know."

Lars Larson walked by. He had a bandage across his nose, a square patch over one eye and a bruise on his cheek. Kathy looked thoughtfully at him. "Vinny, you didn't do all that damage to Lars."

"Who else could have?"

"I saw him leave and he only had one mark on his nose. Something else happened to him last night."

"Okay, but what?" he asked.

"I'll put my network of girl spies out and try to find out," Kathy replied.

Chapter 7

After school Vinny met Kathy and they started for home.

"It was Sam who beat up Lars," Kathy told him. "A girl friend of mine found out. Sam got mad at Lars about something late yesterday afternoon. Two guys held him and Sam started swinging. Looks like Sam got even with Lars for you."

"That still leaves Sam to get."

"What do you mean? You got him already."

"Letting the air out of his tires, you call getting even? I haven't even started."

"Vinny, you'll end up getting yourself killed."

"I'm going to make Sam's life one long headache, from now on. He's been messing me up long enough. It's time he had a turn."

"Speaking of turns, do you suppose *Gooney* is sitting all by herself in the parking lot, unprotected?"

"Damn!" Vinny said and stopped. "I better run. I'll see you tomorrow after I tamper-proof my Ford."

He ran back toward school, cutting past the bike racks to the lot. *Gooney* was still there and beside her stood Jim's Deuce.

"About time you got here, man," Jim said as Vinny ran up. "Sam's red Camaro's been gunning past the lot every couple minutes."

"Now why would Sam do that?" Vinny asked, grinning.

"He wanted to check to see if you had locking valve caps on your tires."

"Thanks, buddy, I appreciate your baby-sitting."

"Vinny, if it's war on Sam, count me in. I want to get in on the fun."

"We'll talk about that later. How did Sam get his flats fixed?"

"Called the Texaco station to come out with a compressor on their pickup. Pumped them up, and zingo!"

"Surprised Sam didn't have a compressor in his trunk."

"I don't know if it's important or not, Vinny, but I heard Sam make a date to go over to Sue Parker's house tonight."

Vinny rubbed his chin. "She lives on Stringtown Road just down from Sixth?" Jim nodded. "Thanks."

"Need any help?"

"Help, Jim? I'll probably be studying hard all evening."

"Come off it, man. You wanta hog all the fun? Let me come help you."

"You're clean, stay that way. But you can come help me work out on the backboard. Basketball season's coming up fast."

They shot baskets until they couldn't see the hoop in the darkness.

The house seemed quiet without his dad's bellowing. Vinny and Hal had sandwiches and leftovers for dinner. Vinny had learned he could cut the grocery bill down four or five dollars a week by eating up the leavings.

After supper Mrs. Walker called to check on her sons. She talked to Hal first.

"Have any homework tonight?"

"Nope."

"How was school today?"

"Fine."

"You must go to bed when Vinny says to."

"Mom, there's a good movie on. Can I stay up till ten to watch it?"

"What is it?"

"The Slimey Monster Serpent from Outer Space!"

"No, Hal, you can't stay up. Now put Vinny on."

Vinny took the phone.

"I'm on my break, Vinny, and thought I'd phone and see how

things are going with your dad gone."

"Going smooth, Mom."

"You be sure to eat enough."

"Sure, Mom."

"Vinny, are you having trouble with Sam White again?"

"Why you ask that?"

"Mr. White had lunch here today. He's got a big mouth. You can hear him all over the place. Answer me, did you have trouble with Sam?"

"Some."

"Vinny, don't fight with that big kid. Let him alone and try to graduate. I see guys in here every day drinking cause they got nothing else to do. Vinny you got to make something of yourself."

"Mom, you ever think how many times you've told me that? Three, maybe four hundred times. I mean if I ain't got the idea by now ...."

"I'm just trying to be a good mother to you, Vinny. Parents make mistakes now and then too, you know."

He let it hang there.

"Vinny, you still on?"

"Yeah, Mom."

"You don't talk to me any more, Vinny. Used to be you'd talk for hours, how you wanted to be an engineer. How you'd get good grades and maybe a scholarship. We're gonna have to talk again, Vinny."

"Sure, Mom, but when? After you get home from work at three a.m.? Maybe Saturday, your one day off, when you do the washing, house cleaning and shopping? When you got any time to talk to me? You ain't got no time!" The more he talked the more upset he got. He wanted to slam down the receiver.

A sniffle came through, then Mrs. Walker spoke again. "Vinny, my break's over, we'll talk again this week-end."

"Sure, Mom."

They said goodbye and hung up. It was Dad's fault not hers. It all came back to Larry Walker, a no-good, falling-down drunk.

Vinny threw a pillow across the room as hard as he could, then switched on the TV.

At nine-thirty he snapped it off and put on his dark clothes again, feeling like a cat-burglar. After checking that Hal was asleep, Vinny borrowed his bike and pedaled six blocks to Sixth Avenue, then left on Stringtown Road. He wasn't sure which house was the Parkers' until he saw Sam's red Camaro parked in front. He stopped half a block away and watched, heart pounding, every muscle taut.

The entire house was alight and a heavy rock beat pulsated up the street from a wide open hi-fi. Although the porchlight was on there was no movement outside. A car headed down the street and Vinny edged into the shadow of a giant oak.

He eased up closer and checked to be sure it was Sam's car. He saw the "White Chevrolet" licence plate frame, and the dent on the passenger's door. It was Sam's. Vinny had no idea what he was going to do. Pull the ignition wires? Swipe the rotor so the car wouldn't run?

He slipped on gloves he had brought with him and studied the red car thoughtfully. It was parked on the wrong side of the street. The window was down. The gentle Stringtown Road grade beckoned. What would happen if he eased off the hand brake, and pushed? There were no houses down that way. The worst it could do would be jump the ditch and bounce off across the field. Sam's old man would fix any damage free in his repair shop, anyway, but it might slow Sam down a little. Sure, it was risky, but it was worth it. What the army guys on TV called a calculated risk.

Vinny checked both directions before he ran past the front of the car to the driver's side. Reaching in the window, he pulled the parking brake release and shifted the car into neutral.

Long slanting headlight beams stabbed at him from downhill. A car was coming up Stringtown. He couldn't roll the Camaro down now! He cramped the front wheels toward the curb and leaned inside the car so no one would recognize him as the vehicle roared past. Vinny breathed a relieved sigh, and turned the wheels away from the curb. It took only a nudge to get the car rolling down the gentle slope. He headed it down the center of the road and let it go.

Vinny ran for his brother's bike and pedaled back up the hill to the turn and stopped to watch as the vehicle swerved to the left, bounced through the ditch and slammed to a stop against an old maple tree halfway down the hill.

He didn't intend it to come out quite like that but Vinny had no regrets as he rode hard back the way he had come. Once he stopped and watched behind a hedge, but no one was following him. He was away clean! The Avenger had struck again, this time right where it hurt!

Chapter 8

Vinny arrived at school ten minutes early the next morning and sat in *Gooney* savoring the sweet taste of revenge.

By noon it was all over school about Sam's wreck. Some of the stories said he totaled the Camaro dragging on Stringtown. Some said it was only a dent in the grille. The average seemed to be that Sam's car had rolled down Stringtown hill, jumped the ditch and hit a tree, smashing the front end in.

Vinny couldn't feel sorry. There was too much of a debt yet to be paid to Sam. It served him right! Now Sam was sweating. Already the kids were razzing him about parking without setting his brakes and Sam wasn't taking it well.

It began raining at mid-morning; lunch would be inside. He saw Kathy just before third period to ask her where they could meet.

She pushed him to one side of the rush, her eyes angry.

"Vinny, you gone crazy? Basketball season's almost here and you're pushing cars down hills? You want to get yourself suspended so you can't play ball? I keep thinking about the fun we can have going to the games, and to the sock-hops after games and all the parties and stuff, and you act dumb-crazy about getting even with somebody!"

She blinked back a tear. "I don't think you like me at all Vinny Walker. If Mom ever got wind of this, poof! there would go the whole romance." She shook her head angrily and stomped away, her hair flying. She was crying.

Vinny stood frozen with amazement. Of all people, he expected

Kathy to understand why he had to get even with Sam. She saw the beating he'd taken. Sam had it coming to him.

Vinny had felt a thrill of revenge when he heard everyone talking about Sam's car. "Sure you put the brake on, Sam. Sure you cramped the wheels, Sam. You always do. Sure, Sam. Sure you put the lever in park position, Sam. Sure!"

Vinny had never seen Sam get so mad. He was yelling in the hall and took off running after one of his tormentors.

Now it all seemed to turn sour in his mouth. He sat through world history wondering about it. Maybe Kathy was right. Maybe he should call it quits. After all, if he got caught he wouldn't be playing basketball and that was even more important than getting Sam. But then he thought about the months of guff he had taken from Sam, and the beating. He decided dumb Sam wasn't even on the books yet. Besides, as long as he didn't do anything foolish on the schoolgrounds, how could they keep him off the team?

On most winter noontimes at Forestville High the gym was opened for socks-only basketball games. After lunch Vinny and Jim went to the gym and got in a game. He felt good on the court, and even in socks Vinny hit half of his corner jump shots.

Lars was on the court. Despite the beating Lars had given him, Vinny couldn't work up any hatred. If Sam and Lars had fought, there might be more to it than he knew. Lars was an excellent ball handler, better than most of the varsity players last year. If Lars turned out he looked like a cinch for the varsity squad.

Vinny thought about who Forestville had left in basketball. Three lettermen were back at forward, one center and one guard. If he wanted to try for a guard spot he might have an easier time than at forward. That meant he had to keep up his running.

Another thought came to him as he passed off to Jim, who made a lay-up just as the ten-minute warning bell sounded. Three of those five returning lettermen were seniors and all were good buddies of Sam. Two had played football with him. That could lead to trouble on a team. Vinny scowled thinking about it as he and Jim ran for class.

That afternoon Vinny couldn't find Kathy. She must have left for home straight from her last class without going to her locker. At least the rain had stopped.

When he got to his car the right rear tire was flat. The valve cap was on, he had tightened them all with pliers. A round hole showed on the sidewall where a nail or an ice pick had been used. *Sam White strikes back*, Vinny thought. It took him fifteen minutes to change the tire. He threw the dead one in the trunk and drove home warily. He couldn't afford to have another flat before he had that one fixed. He'd have to run without a spare or leave *Gooney* home. He decided to let her sit a while. It would be cheaper, and he needed the workout, running to and from school.

At home Vinny stripped and put on a pair of track shorts, tennis shoes and sweatshirt. He ran around the block four times covering over two miles. When he came back to the garage he felt relaxed and loose. Another forty-five minutes for jump shots, then Vinny concentrated on bouncing he ball off the garage door, grabbing it and shooting fast, pretending each time he was shooting over big superstar, Wilt Chamberlain.

With his dad in jail, things settled into a steady predictable routine at home. It rained Thursday and Friday and Vinny didn't see Kathy either day. She never seemed to be at her locker, nor in the cafeteria. He didn't like to think about it but he guessed they were through.

He ran half-way to school each morning, walking the last mile so he wouldn't sweat too much. After school he ran the two miles home, then followed his regular workout of shooting and dribbling. He had to be in shape, basketball tryouts were set for the following Monday.

Only one disturbing thing happened, and that didn't affect Vinny directly. Friday night at the last football game of the season, Sam showed up in a brand new blue Camaro to replace the smashed one. Vinny burned, but to balance the books, Sam White, the football superstar, missed two important blocks which caused Forestville to lose their last game of the season, 27-14.

Basketball tryouts were held Monday right after school. Over eighty boys crowded the bleacher seats. The stands were marked in four sections: last year's varsity, last year's JV, last year's frosh squad and a fourth part labeled "raw material."

The coach gave a short talk about how only a few boys could play basketball; not more than seventeen on each team, so a lot of them would be disappointed. Then he had the "raw material" section suit up and start practicing. The coaches wrote down names on clipboards, and ran dribbling, passing and shooting tests.

Lars looked great. He was sure to make varsity.

After an hour and a half the workout split, with the JV squad going to one end and the frosh from last year to the other. The five varsity lettermen assisted the coaches.

Coach Farley worked with the former JV players.

"Okay you guys, move it out two laps around the gym. Go, now!" They went, pounding around hard and fast, coming back panting.

"Two lines for lay-ups, right side shoots, let's go."

He ran them through training drills for another thirty minutes.

"Anybody here a senior?" Farley asked.

One boy held up his hand. The coach talked with him and he sat down.

"How many juniors?" There were five. They grouped around Coach Farley. "We usually don't use juniors on the JV. You five sit down over there and we'll try you tomorrow night with the varsity. We've got a lot of holes to fill this year."

They sat down. Vinny felt elated. He had a real chance to make it! A shot at the varsity! Wait until he told Kathy. Maybe he should call her tonight.

Vinny ran home without stopping. It was nearly six when he came into the house. Hal was watching TV.

After dinner Vinny did his math, then called Kathy.

"This is the Bell residence," a woman's voice answered.

"Could I speak with Kathy, please?"

"Who is calling?"

"Vinny Walker."

There was a pause, he was afraid she was going to say, "No town drunk's kid can talk to my little girl," but she didn't. "I'll see if she's here."

"I'm here, Mom. Hi, Vinny."

"Hi, Kathy."

There was a long silence.

"Mother, are you *ever* going to put down the phone?"

Vinny heard a sharp intake of breath and a click.

"Sorry about that, Vinny. Been hoping you'd call."

"I tried out for the team. I think I got a good chance of making the varsity!"

"Yippee! That's simply tremendous! Wait till I tell the girls at school tomorrow. Golly, Vinny, that's just great!"

"You still mad at me?"

"No. I was just scared you'd do something dumb and get suspended. Now that you know you can make the team everything's great. You *are* gonna forget all about old Sam, right?"

"Let's talk about it at lunch tomorrow, okay?" Vinny hedged.

"Sure, Vinny! But stay away from Sam, please?"

She waited for his assurance. Neither of them said anything for a while, just listened to each other breathe through the phone.

"Vinny?"

"Yeah?"

"I'm really glad you called. I've missed seeing you."

"Me, too."

"You still hate Sam, don't you?"

"Yes."

"Why? I mean why so much?"

"A lot of reasons, Kathy. He's got money and a brand new car. He's a big letterman, his dad's got the big car dealership. *And* he's been riding me for months now about my dad."

"But most because of what he says about your dad?"

"That, most of all."

"Stay away from him, Vinny," Kathy pleaded. "Please? You drop that and everything will be groovy. We can even go steady, Vinny!"

Vinny's heart gave a flip. Go steady! Wow! But he'd have t

honest with Kathy.

"I'm not through with Sam yet, Kathy. He stuck an icepick in *Gooney's* tire. I got to square that count."

"Vinny, you're so damned stubborn. You're gonna spoil everything."

"Let's talk about it at lunch tomorrow," Vinny offered.

"No, Vinny. We've talked about it enough. You know how I feel."

She slammed the phone in his ear. Damn Sam White! He was screwing up everything.

Vinny hustled Hal to bed and made certain he was sleeping. As he dressed in his Black Avenger uniform he remembered when he wore the pants and T-shirt last, and the thrill of watching Sam's car rolling down the hill. He had nothing so dramatic planned for tonight. He slipped an ice pick, a screwdriver and a six-inch crescent wrench into his pockets.

A few minutes later Vinny pedaled toward Sam's house. He rode past twice on his bike. No one seemed to be at home. It was all blacked out. There was no blue Camaro sitting out in front or in the drive. The garage door was down. In a week or two the newness would wear off the car, and Sam would get careless and start leaving it parked in the driveway again, then he'd fix it.

A car came slowly around the far corner of the block, and Vinny recognized the white city police cruiser. He pushed the bike against the hedge and stepped behind it.

The spotlight stabbed into the bushes around the house as the prowl car passed, and continued to probe the shadows until it was well past the White place. As it passed where he hid Vinny could hear the radio speaker.

When the cruiser rounded the corner, Vinny rode home on the sidewalks, taking backstreets, avoiding the lights.

His knees were weak as he parked Hal's bike at home and let himself in the back door with his key. If that new cop had caught him close to the White's house he would have had a tough time explaining why he was there with an icepick in his pocket.

Chapter 9

Tuesday afternoon varsity basketball practice began. Twenty-two apprehensive boys suited up.

Vinny looked at the prospects. The five varsity lettermen had on practice uniforms, the rest wore gym shorts and T-shirts. Coach Farley came out swinging a whistle and yelled, "Five laps around the court, and stay outside the lines. Go!"

Vinny wasn't even breathing hard as he finished the run. All his running to and from school had paid off. They did four or five simple exercises to loosen up, then gathered around the coach.

"Now listen closely. If you want to play basketball for me you'll have to work hard. We're a running team, and I like to see plenty of hustle. Each of you will have a chance to make the team. If you don't make it, I don't want any griping. We'll carry seventeen players, so five of you will be cut. The JV can take three more players and anybody who gets cut here can try there. Any questions?"

There weren't. He split the group into three squads and put two of them on the floor. Each of the varsity players had a clipboard; so did the three coaches.

"Pick your positions, we'll have a ten-minute regulation game. No fouls called but we'll be counting them on our boards. Work together and let's see if any of you can play basketball."

It was a madhouse. Vinny went to a forward position when his team had three guards. Lars Larson was on the other team Everyone hogged the ball, trying to show the coaches that he co score. Vinny worked hard on defense, took four rebounds and hit on five jumpers from fifteen feet out along the back boundary line.

It was rough-and-tumble basketball, but no whistle blew. One of the boys sagged and left the court midway in the game. He struggled to the edge of the court and threw up. Vinny was getting tired, but not all that pooped. He ended the game with a jumper that missed as the whistle blew.

Five boys from the first two squads were picked to take on the remaining five untested players. Lars and Vinny both got the nod. The five tired boys slowed the game down this time, passing to each other more, working together, and trying for simple set ups and screens. The coach called it after five minutes. The seventeen sat on the bench and watched the varsity five work out with some of last year's drills and patterns.

For the final test each player had twenty shots from the free throw line. Bull Knapp, veteran center for Forestville, hit twenty in a row. He was six-foot-three and weighed two hundred and twenty, but he could move like a guard. One of the new boys hit only three of twenty. Vinny canned the first twelve, then missed one and hit six of the last seven for eighteen. He was second high.

When practice ended a bunch of very tired boys headed for the showers. Vinny found Lars sitting beside him in front of their lockers when he went to dress.

"You've played some basketball before," Lars said.

"Some."

"You're a lot better at it than boxing," Lars said, grinning.

Vinny laughed. He had wondered who would mention the fight first and how it would happen. He was relieved that it was over.

"Boxing's not my thing. Too bad we don't have a boxing team here at school."

"Yeah. I was on a Y boxing team where I used to live. Say, that jumper of yours is good, Vinny. Keep dunking it," Lars said as he got up to leave. Vinny had wanted to ask him what happened between him and Sam but had missed his chance.

The next two days Coach Farley worked them hard. He would post the cut list Thursday morning, he said. Vinny tried harder than he ever had in his life. He learned how to dribble automatically, letting the ball touch only the tips of his fingers, watching the other players as he came down the court, setting up plays, running, cutting, passing.

He concentrated on the dribbling practice, thinking he might have to work as a guard, but he quickly saw that only three of the varsity players would start. That included only one forward.

Vinny hadn't thought about Sam for three days. He was full of basketball, and wanted to make the team more than anything else in the world.

Thursday morning Vinny checked the bulletin board at the gym. The typed varsity squad was posted. His eyes darted down the list, Knapp, Larson, Walker, *WALKER! He had survived the cut, he was on the varsity squad!* Vinny threw his history book high in the air.

"Yaaaaaahooooooo!" he yelled, and barely caught the book as it came down. His first thoughts were of Kathy. He ran to the quad and looked down the street toward her house.

He waited until the five-minute bell, still Kathy hadn't come. Right after his class he ran toward her locker. Halfway down the hall he saw her headed his way.

"Kathy?" He wanted to pick her up and whirl her around, he was so excited.

"I heard you made the varsity!" she beamed.

"Yeah," he said excitedly. "Kathy, I think that's the first time anybody's heard anything good about me."

"It's just the start of a long list of good things, Vinny. I know." She touched his arm. "Lunch? Cafeteria?"

He nodded eagerly. "I've got to run," she said.

He watched her go, straight and tall, brown hair bouncing as she walked. *A long list of good things*, Kathy had said. He hoped so.

Practice that night settled down to Coach Farley's pattern: run, exercise, run again, then drill, drill, shoot and drill some more.

Immediately, Vinny found himself on the receiving end of Coach Farley's slashing criticism.

"No, no, no! Walker. Dribble lower, keep the bounce shorter

and harder. Fingertips, fingertips! That's better. Now watch and move as you dribble, or you'll get stripped from behind. No, no! Go around him, that's charging!"

Each time he had the ball the coach was all over him, but each time Vinny thought it through and knew the coach was right. In drills they worked hard on two-on-one for the fast break. It meant running full-court passing the ball back and forth and setting up one of the two men for a sure shot at the home basket. Twice Vinny messed up the charge down the floor when it came his turn by dropping a pass or making a bad throw.

"Walker, you've got to move and look, dribble and run, and when you don't have the ball, fake your man out so you can break for the basket."

Friday night the workout was tougher, and again Vinny caught more than his share of guff from the coach. Before he let them go the coach called them around him.

"You guys call yourselves basketball players? I know a church team that could beat you!" His snarl turned off and he grinned. "Not too many though. We're coming along."

"We've got just six more school days to practice before our first game with Crawford High. We need two weeks. You know according to the league rules we can't practice on Saturday or Sunday." He smiled. "But, I've talked to the principal and we're opening the gym to community recreation both days. The gym will be open at nine tomorrow morning until five, and open from noon Sunday until eight in the evening. According to league rules, I can't be here, but it sure would be fine if you boys came out," he hinted broadly.

The next ten days Vinny breathed basketball. Every chance he got he had a ball in his hands, dribbling, shooting, passing. Monday night before the game they eased off the drills, concentrated on shooting.

Coach Farley stopped them about four. "That's enough. I want each of you to get ten hours of sleep tonight. So get home and eat and go to bed. Report at six-thirty tomorrow night."

Vinny tried. He went to bed at nine-thirty, but he couldn't sleep. He was so excited he couldn't lie still. He had finally realized this week why Coach Farley had been riding him so hard. The coach might start him! He could be on the starting lineup at forward! Vinny jumped out of bed and went into the living room to watch TV. It didn't interest him. Starting a game would show Sam that Vinny Walker was as good as he was any day!

Wide awake, he wondered where Sam's new Camaro was. He jumped up and ran back to his room. Ten minutes later he pedaled into the deep shadow just down the street from Sam's house. The Camaro sat in the driveway, its wide-track tires beckoning.

Vinny jammed the ice pick through the back tire sidewall. It was surprisingly easy. He pulled the tool out and heard the hiss of air.

That evens the score on ice-picked tires, Sam, Vinny thought.

Chapter 10

Vinny was so excited he couldn't wait any longer. He left *Gooney* two blocks from Kathy's and jogged there. He was early for their date, but she was ready.

Hand in hand, they half-ran to the big gymnasium. What a transformation had taken place! This morning it was just another school building. Now it was draped with bright maroon and gold rosettes with twisted streamers festooned between them. Discordant sounds of the pep band tuning up added to the electrifying atmosphere. The excitement and anticipation of the *first big game* crackled in the air.

Vinny squeezed Kathy's hand. "Wait here a minute while I check in with the coach," he said.

Kathy held his arm tightly when he returned and sat beside her.

"It's happening, Vinny. Remember when I said you would be hearing all sorts of good things about yourself? Three girls behind me were simply raving about you while you were gone. I told them you were my date and not to get any ideas. They were all juniors, too."

Vinny grinned. "That's basketball power! I've waited a long time for this." He took her hand and she leaned close against him possessively.

At the end of the first half, Vinny stood up.

"See you right here, after the game. It'll take me about ten minutes to get showered and dressed, so don't run off."

"I'll be here," she said, squeezing his hand. "Good luck, Vinny!"

There was so much excitement in the locker room that the air seemed to prickle his skin. When the equipment manager issued his game uniform, Vinny shivered. He had dreamed of wearing the maroon and gold of the Viking varsity for so long! The varsity! He put on the shorts and shirt and then the warm-up pants and jacket. The players stretched full length on benches in front of lockers, resting, trying to keep their guts from knotting up. During the last two minutes of the JV game, the coach called them together.

"Our first game is strictly a practice session," he began, "so don't get too up-tight. I'm going to see what a lot of you can do in an actual game tonight. Naturally, we want to win, but I might pull somebody who is doing well to try somebody else so don't think you flubbed if you get pulled. Remember this is a team sport. Teamwork is what wins basketball games, so don't play ball-hog or you'll be riding the bench. Now be ready to take the floor as soon as the JV's come in. I'll set the starters just before the game."

Vinny was sweating yet cold at the same time. Chills chased each other up his spine. The ankle-length suit was hot. In the next moment he forgot about himself as the locker room door burst open and a jubilant, winning JV horde poured in. The varsity waited for them to pass, then surged out the door with Bull Knapp leading the way and the coach bringing up the rear.

The roof of Forestville High gym shook as the cheering squad pumped the crowd into action. Six basketballs bombarded the hoop as the sixteen maroon and gold teammates shot. They quickly moved into a lay-up drill, and a weave. Then the balls were back and it was every man for himself to twang the hemp cord below the basket.

After a fast ten minutes of practice, the coach walked out and nodded to Bull, then to Johnny Sinclair and Paul Vandering. All three took off their warm-ups. They were starting. The coach watched the test before tapping Dave Eldridge on the shoulder. Vinny got a ball and jumped, his shot swishing through the hoop.

"Okay, Vinny, take off your gear, you're starting at forward."

Vinny grinned and unzipped his jacket. The long pants came

off, and Vinny was under the basket with the other starters.

Bull gave Vinny a strange look but didn't say anything. The whistle sounded and the team took its place at the center of the court for the national anthem. Vinny didn't even hear the pep band play the music. When it was over he moved into his position nearest his basket and shook hands with the Crawford High player.

Bull Knapp won the jump, tipped the ball to the other forward Paul Vandering and the game was on. It took Vinny a few seconds to realize *this was it*. This was his first varsity game! By that time Paul had worked the ball to Knapp who tried a ten-footer and missed. Vinny raced down court to his position, going into a man-to-man defense.

Twice his man got the ball, but Vinny refused to let him go around or shoot. One of their guards took a twenty foot set-shot and dunked it. Crawford 2, Forestville 0.

The fourth time Forestville had the ball, Vinny realized he had never touched it. They were playing freeze-out, and he was sure they had no intention of passing to him. He worked closer to the basket, nearer to the three-second-line lane, and on the next shot he was in position to clear the board and drop in a ten foot fall-away shot.

When the Forestville Vikings got control again Coach Farley signaled to Sinclair to call time out.

"What's going on out there?" Farley asked, his voice shrill with anger. "You guys playing a four-man team? Why don't you use Walker?"

"He just ain't open, Coach," Sinclair said.

"He's not working the patterns," Knapp said.

"You guys think I'm blind? I know he's been open. Now get some passing going and start the fast break, or I'm going to bench all five of you."

Vinny played it very loose, ten feet from his best position toward the corner. Three times Sinclair and Eldridge dribbled past him rather than pass. Vinny saw Eldridge steal the ball as Crawford High brought it down the court, and he broke fast. Eldridge slowed it down again, killing the fast break. Coach Farley was on his feet, hands on his hips.

Vinny came out in perfect position for the high post inside cross and Knapp ignored him, giving off to Vandering who shot and missed. Vinny followed, got the rebound and dribbled out of traffic to his corner. He faked a pass to Sinclair, jumped and swished a twenty-footer.

Crawford called time and both teams trotted to their benches. Coach Farley made three substitutions, Vinny and the two guards. Forestville was behind 14-8.

The coach said only one thing to the new team. "You have five men out there, now use them all and play ball!"

Vinny sat on the bench, a jacket draped around his shoulders. Knapp, Sinclair and Eldridge, the three buddies of Sam White, had saved their little surprise for the opening game. It would be the same way all season! How could he play basketball if no one passed the ball to him!

The coach couldn't buck all four of them. He would bench Vinny, not his four best players. They simply didn't have anyone else who could play center. And from what Vinny had seen, Bull Knapp was the key man in the freeze-out plot.

Forestville began putting points on the board. Lars had moved in at guard and fired the team. Bull worked both forwards and both guards and when they played him too loose, he dunked short ones. By the end of the first eight-minute quarter, the home team had pulled to within two points of a tie.

At the break between quarters Coach Farley changed his line-up. Vinny went back at forward and Sinclair at guard. That left Lars still at the other guard position and Knapp at center, Vandering at the other forward.

"Let's try this combination. Move the ball around. Pass them crazy and work both those forwards!"

It was a re-run of the first quarter with the exception that Lars passed to Vinny. No one else did. Vinny worked the boards, getting three more rebounds and dropping two of them for buckets. At the half Crawford was in the lead 38-26.

Inside the locker room the door was locked and Coach Farley

glared at the players, his hands on his hips.

"You guys really think I'm that dumb, don't you? You think I don't know what's going on around here? I thought you'd outgrown kid tricks like this. I bet you guys still wet your pants and get scared of the dark!" He walked the length of the room and came back, his face black with anger, his voice cold and low, but every word came through, clear.

"When you come in that locker room door and put on that uniform, you leave all your petty gripes and fights outside! If you want me to name names and dates I can. I know about a fight in a park, and about a car with four flats. I know a hell of a lot more than you creeps give me credit for. I keep my ear to the ground.

"This second half we're going to play basketball, not politics. If I see anybody trying any cute tricks, that player gets benched for the rest of the game; maybe for the rest of the season. I'm coaching this team. If you don't think so, turn in your uniform right now and clear out!"

Nobody moved; nobody spoke. Vinny let his breath out slowly. He hadn't realized he'd been holding it.

"This second half we're going to use our fast break and the full court press. So lay down and rest."

Before Vinny's stomach unknotted, the knock came on the door and he hustled out for the second half. He started again. They ran, they pressed, they worked as a team. By the middle of the fourth quarter Forestville High had pulled within four points. It was like practice, everyone working together, playing team ball. Coach Farley signaled Sinclair to call a time out.

"That's more like playing the game," he said. He substituted an entirely new team to give more of the boys a try under fire. The Crawford coach substituted too, clearing his bench. Crawford hung on to win by four points.

Coach Farley always made a short evaluation after each game. The boys gathered around him in the locker room.

"The second half we played some ball. That's all we're going to play from now on. Get home and get some sleep, I'm gonna run your tails off tomorrow."

Chapter 11

Vinny saw Bull Knapp talking with the coach after the game. When he came from his shower, he noticed Sinclair in the cage. As he finished dressing the coach called him.

Vinny sat down on the bench before the coach.

"Yes sir?"

"It was like I figured, Walker. Four of my starters were playing a cute little game, just as a joke."

"Some joke."

"Right. How do you feel about tonight's game?"

"We had a good second half."

"What about the first half, how did you like the game of keep-away?"

"I got mad, Coach. My first game and they wouldn't pass to me. The longer it went on the madder I got. I thought about quitting right then. I figured after this you'd probably have me riding the bench most of the time."

"You're not riding the bench, Walker. You're my starter, and you're going to stay there as long as you play heads-up ball." The coach rubbed his hands over his face as he caught his rising anger. "You've got good hands, Walker, and ability, the *feel* for the game. You take coaching well, and you aren't afraid to work. Now get out of here."

Vinny wondered what the coach had said to the other starters. He put the rest of his gear into his locker and ran for the door. He saw Kathy at the far end of the gym near the door. Lars was with her.

"Nice game, Vinny!" Kathy said grabbing his arm as he ran up. "I was all alone so I asked Lars to wait with me until you came."

"Hardest job I've had all week," Lars said grinning.

They went out into the raw December night. Lars waved and started walking away.

"Hey, Lars, give you a lift home? Got my wheels down the block."

Lars turned. "Thanks, I'm beat."

"You're the best guard on the team, Lars," Vinny said. "You should be starting."

Lars shrugged and walked with them toward *Gooney.* They talked about the freeze-out.

"That was dirty pool," Lars said. "I like a good fair fight, but that was gutter stuff."

They were half a block from the car near a vacant lot when Sam White stepped from behind a tree.

"Vinny Walker, you sonuvabitch!" Sam growled. "You ruined one of my wide-boot tires last night!"

Vinny pushed Kathy behind him as Sam came forward. When Sam stepped out of the shadows Vinny saw the deadly, foot-long piece of pipe in his hand.

"I've had it with you, Walker. You've messed up my car for the last time. You wrecked my old Camaro, too. I'm settling up, right now."

He moved forward.

"Smart, very smart, Sam." Vinny faked a laugh. "You big, dumb freak! Coming at me with a lead pipe. That's assault with a deadly weapon. I've got two witnesses. They'll throw the key away if you touch me, Sam. Think your dad could buy off a judge and a whole jury?"

Sam kept coming. They could see he was so fighting mad he couldn't think straight. "Get out of here Kathy," Vinny said as he pushed her away.

"Put it down, Sam. You on a trip again? You look like you're on the stuff," Lars said.

Sam was a lineman now, coming at a halfback. Vinny backed

up, trying to get a tree between them. He had to wait until Kathy was far enough away, then he would run. It would be suicide to go against Sam and that lead pipe.

Sam rushed him. Vinny saw movement to his left and suddenly Lars sprang st Sam, feet first, kicking him in the stomach with both feet. As Lars dropped to the ground he rolled over and sprang back to his feet in a continuous movement, ready to launch another attack. It wasn't necessary. Sam crumpled, dropping the pipe, gasping for breath, his solar plexus paralyzed.

Lars picked up the pipe and threw it to the far side of the lot.

Kathy hurried back to meet them.

Five minutes later the three of them piled into *Gooney* and drove her to the far side of Kathy's block.

Vinny reached for his door handle when Kathy leaned over and whispered, "Aren't you going to drop Lars off first?"

He grinned and nodded.

He started *Gooney* up again and looked across Kathy at Lars. "I don't even know where you live, man."

Lars told him and Vinny laughed.

"What's so funny?"

"If anybody told me two weeks ago I'd be giving you a ride home, I'd have clubbed him."

"I was new in town."

"Yeah, and what a right hand! Where did you learn that foot fighting stuff?"

"I took some karate classes. It comes in handy when you can't get to a big guy any other way."

"Especially when he's got a lead pipe."

Lars lived only six blocks from Vinny. When the car stopped Vinny offered Lars his hand.

"Lars, thanks again for putting down Sam. If you're keeping track, that more than balances out our books."

Lars laughed. "Forget it, Vinny. We both may have to work over Bull Knapp next." He waved and ran toward the house.

As Vinny drove, Kathy snuggled beside him. Vinny put his free arm around her shoulder and pulled her tightly against him.

He parked a half block from her house, and turned off the engine.

"Vinny, I'm so proud of you!" she said. "I'm thrilled you're on the varsity and that I'm your girl. I am your girl, aren't I?"

She held her face up to him and Vinny kissed her awkwardly. She sighed and he kissed her again and she clung to him a moment, then pushed away.

"I better vanish, you big Viking varsity basketball player. It's been groovy, and this is just the start. We're gonna have a time!"

Vinny went around the car, helped her out, and walked her to the door.

"See you tomorrow," she said as she went into the house.

Vinny ran back to the car and fired the mill. He had to be careful driving home. What a blast! His first game, his first girl! Everything was perfect! Except Sam, but he'd worry about Sam when the time came. Maybe after tonight he would leave Vinny alone.

When Vinny got home he smelled something hatefully familiar. His dad was home again. He had forgotten he was due out of jail today.

He checked the living room and bedroom, and found him on the bathroom floor. Vomit splattered half the floor and the sink. Vinny gagged but kept his own stomach from erupting, as he dragged his father into the hall and wiped his face and arms clean with a wet towel. He pulled him on into his parents' bedroom and threw a blanket over him. He worked half an hour cleaning the bathroom and washing the towels.

Where did he get the booze? Coming out of jail he wouldn't have any money, and usually the cops brought him home. Vinny could only guess he had talked the police into letting him stay downtown and had panhandled his way to a roaring drunk. Looking presentable after a dry month, he must have hit a generous sucker.

Vinny couldn't understand it. He knew that most drunks kept promising to dry out and get a job, but his dad never did. He whined and argued, but he never promised to stop drinking.

From now on I'm gonna be a regular Carrie Nation, Vinny vowed. He would break every bottle he saw in the house and dump out every can of beer! He was sick of cleaning up after his old man.

Chapter 12

Larry Walker blinked at the sun and looked across the street at the Shell service station. Hell, he'd give it a try. Dutch Van Dyke had gone to the trouble to get him the job, least he could do was try it. Larry didn't like cars, but the only jobs he'd had in the past four years had been in filling stations.

He walked across the street, wishing his head would stop hurting. Thirtty days without a drop of booze left the old system unprepared for the barrage of whiskey and beer he'd swilled yesterday.

"Joe Carney?" he asked, looking at the smaller man.

"Right. Larry Walker?" Joe held out his hand.

"You've worked gas stations before, Larry. All I want you to do is pump gas and add a quart of oil now and then. I get lots of repair work, and I like to stay in the shop."

Larry nodded. Joe showed him how to use the pumps and to write up charge tickets.

"Got it Larry?"

"Uh, oh, yeah, got it." His stomach churned and his head pounded. He shoved his hands into his pockets so Joe wouldn't see how badly they were shaking. He wasn't going to like it, he knew, for the smell of gasoline fumes sickened him.

An hour later Larry Walker was shuffling home. He didn't know how it had happened. One minute he was adding a quart of oil to a Chevy, and the next the whole engine was on fire.

Joe charged out with an extinguisher and doused the flames before anything exploded. Then he looked at the engine and shook his head. He would have to rent an identical car from the White Chevy agency to loan this guy while he fixed the burned-up car. A lot of wiring was gone and the distributor leads ruined.

"Larry, I told you not to smoke while you're pumping gas or working under the hood," Joe said. "Only thing I can figure is an ash dropped into some gasoline or a spark lit some oil and it flashed up in your face."

"Sorry, Joe, it won't happen again."

Joe Carney shook his head. He had hoped to give the Walker family a little boost with this job.

"Sorry, Larry, but it won't work. We were lucky the whole place didn't blow sky high."

Vinny heard about it at school during lunch. They were eating outside when a girl from his English class told them about the fire at Joe Carney's. Vinny was sure his father was the cause of it. As she left, Sam White and Bull Knapp walked by slowly. Sam never looked at Vinny as he talked to Bull.

"Hey, Bull, hear about our town drunk's last bit? He set fire to a car down at Carney's Shell Station. Joe should have known better than to hire that drunk!"

They laughed and moved on. Vinny balled his fists with frustration. He wanted to run after Sam and slam him one, but his better sense prevailed. He tried to think about the team. He was a first string, a *basketball starter!* He told himself, *Don't throw it all down the drain now!* Kathy's hand on his helped.

"Let's go for a walk," she said and led him away from the rest of the kids. She steered him toward the parking lot, chattering all the while.

"So these two girls in English asked me how many points you made in the game last night. I said sixteen and they thought fourteen, how many was it?"

He didn't answer.

"Vinny, how many points did you make last night?"

"Huh? Oh, yeah, sixteen."

"Hey, I felt pretty important this morning. I mean, going to the game with the star player. You're really going to set the team on fire, right?" She waited for a reply but he paid no attention.

"Vinny?"

"Uh, oh, what, Kathy?"

"You're mad and I don't blame you. I mean, I'm no brain, but how does a girl tell someone she likes to be careful? Vinny, please don't blow it and spoil the whole season."

"Kathy, maybe I've been too careful. Maybe Sam is the kind of guy you have to beat the hell out of before he'll let you alone."

He remained silent for a while and Kathy sensed his need to sort out his thoughts. "I want to play ball, Kathy. I've worked all fall getting ready, but if Sam keeps bugging me, I'll take him on, anyway. I'm not letting Sam push my face in the dirt just so I can go on playing basketball! Do you understand, Kathy?"

"But you can't win, Vinny. If you fight him on the school grounds, you'll get suspended whether you win or lose."

She didn't understand, or didn't want to. As he saw it, he didn't have a choice. It was a matter of honor.

No one mentioned his father's latest escapade the rest of the day. Still Vinny felt relieved when the final bell rang.

"So far, so good," he told Kathy as they crossed the street, heading home. She had waited for him in the library until basketball workout was over.

They walked slowly, in no hurry to cover the three blocks. Kathy saw them first: the three lettermen blocking the sidewalk just beyond the vacant lot where Sam waylaid them last night. Only this time he'd brought reinforcements.

Sam stood in the middle with Bull Knapp on one side and Johnny Sinclair on the other.

"Here's the town drunk's kid and his whore," Sam said.

"No, Sam, you got it wrong," Sinclair said. "He's only the town drunk's kid, it's his *mother* who's the whore."

"Ain't he a mess? They shoulda run his family out of town years ago," Sam said.

Vinny felt his chest tighten as his heart raced.

"Come on, Vinny," Kathy said, grabbing his arm. "Let's go the other way."

"No, Kathy. We're off the school grounds now," Vinny said, darting toward the two, aiming at Sinclair. At the last minute he shifted, slamming into Sam. Vinny hit him with his forearms like a football blocker, and Sam, surprised, stumbled back as Vinny's one hundred sixty pounds smashed into him. He fell backwards, rolled to one side and came to his feet quickly.

Vinny held his ground and turned toward Sinclair.

"You really want in this, Sinclair?"

"You're damned right."

Vinny drove in, bouncing his fist off Sinclair's jaw and taking one to the stomach. Sinclair wheeled as Sam spun Vinny around with a clout to his shoulder.

"You're in good form, Sam, two against one," Vinny gasped.

"This ain't a fight," Sam grated. "I'm planning to fix you for good, Walker."

Knapp stayed out of it, but he'd be there too if Sam needed help.

Vinny backed into the vacant lot trying to keep his back toward the hedgerow. He could avoid Sam's charges, but the combination of attacks began to tell. Sinclair caught his cheek with a solid smash, dazing Vinny, and Sam stepped in and plowed a big fist into Vinny's stomach. He fell backwards. Sinclair stepped back, but Sam drove in trying to kick Vinny in the stomach. He saw the foot coming, caught it and pulled. Sam lost his balance and lay in the dirt.

Vinny jumped up and charged Sinclair, who was standing watching Sam. The charge carried Sinclair straight back into an oak tree. His head hit the tree hard and Vinny felt him go limp and watched him slide down the trunk to the ground. His eyes rolled back.

Sam heard Sinclair's head thunk against the tree and saw his fallen form. Suddenly the fight was over.

"You killed him, Walker," said Bull, bending over Sinclair.

Vinny looked at Sinclair. He still hadn't moved. He lifted one of his hands and let it fall, limply. “He's faking, he just bumped his head a little.”

Sam knelt beside him and slapped both Sinclair's cheeks. Then stood and looked at Vinny.

“This is better than beating up on you, Walker. You hurt John bad. The cops will get you now, sure. Bull, call the cops, go next door. Call an ambulance too.”

Vinny looked for Kathy. She had waited down the block, so he ran to her.

“Is he hurt bad, Vinny?”

“Naw, he couldn't be, just knocked out,” Vinny said. But a trace of doubt crept into his voice.

“I'm scared, I can't help it!”

“Don't worry, he isn't hurt bad, and we're off campus so the school can't touch me.” Vinny said it confidently, but he was starting to wonder. What if Sinclair really was hurt bad? What if his old man wanted to press charges? What did they call it, assault? Was that a felony? It didn't matter. Whatever it was, they had him, but good.

Chapter 13

Vinny sat on the hard chair in the principal's office. It was eight-thirty p.m. and they were still talking. The school board was meeting in special session talking to Sam White and Bull Knapp and Kathy. It would be his turn soon.

This morning he heard Sinclair was in the hospital with a skull fracture. He would be there for a while, and couldn't play basketball or take part in any sports for the rest of the year.

Vinny had waited fourth and fifth periods for the call from the vice-principal's office. Finally, just before basketball practice he went in to the office. The secretary said that Mr. Johnson had been trying to find him.

The vice-principal explained that technically the school had jurisdiction over students until they reached their homes after school. Since none of them had been home, the fight was considered to be within the school's jurisdiction.

Now he sat in the office, waiting for the school board to complete its hearing. Vinny stared at the pictures on the wall. When would they let him tell what happened?

Ten minutes later the door opened and the secretary nodded for him to come in.

Vinny knew none of the board members. The chairman was a man he had seen around town, Mr. Green, a real estate man.

"Sit down, Walker. You know why we're here, and what this is all about. What we want you to do is tell us, in your own words, exactly what happened yesterday after baseball practice. This isn't a trial, we're only trying to get the facts."

He told them exactly how it was; that Sam and Johnny Sinclair had called his mother and Kathy whores, and that he was justified in defending them.

"Mr. Green. That's how it happened. It was an accident. And I don't think there's a person here who wouldn't have done the same if *their* mothers or daughters were called nasty names. I'm sorry Sinclair is hurt, but there were two of them on me and I had to defend myself. He and Sam White started it, not me. They're the ones who should be punished."

There were no more questions from the board. Vinny looked around and saw Kathy and Coach Farley. Kathy, sitting beside her mother, smiled at him weakly. She looked scared. Coach Farley nodded. Then everyone except the board members and the principal were asked to leave.

Mrs. Bell kept Kathy cornered at the far end of the hall as they waited. Vinny talked to his mother who had come from work for the meeting. Coach Farley came over, said hello to his mom and shook her hand.

"It's going to be okay, Vinny," the coach said. "Two to one, anyone can see you wouldn't go into a fight with those odds unless you were forced."

It took the board only five minutes, then everyone was called back in. Mr. Green made the announcement.

"The board has considered all the facts here and has come to a decision. We feel the continual harassment of Vincent Walker by several students is unfortunate and in extremely bad taste. We concur in the opinion that Sam White is responsible for the fight and he is suspended for five consecutive school days. John Sinclair is also suspended for five days."

"Because of his previous record of fighting, and with the suggestion that he was not forced to participate in the fight, we also must suspend Vincent Walker for five days."

"What?" Vinny shouted, jumping to his feet. "Two guys try to beat me up and *I* get suspended!"

A strong hand pushed him down into his seat. It was Coach Farley.

"Mr. Green, it does seem unusual the victim of an assault gets the same punishment as the attackers. I'll have to protest your decision and ask the board to reconsider."

Mr. Green was still standing. He looked surprised, but when he spoke, his voice was conciliatory.

"Coach Farley, we know you're interested in this boy, and what you said helped his cause, but we're thinking of his own good as well. We believe a little firm discipline now will help straighten him out."

"Like hell you do!" Vinny shouted as he pushed to his feet. "You and the whole stinking school board are afraid of Sam's dad. The town knows Wilbur White pulls the strings around here. Why don't you just send me to the reform school and forget it? You can all go to hell as far as I care!"

He fled the room, slamming the door hard. He ran out of the building to *Gooney* before anyone could stop him.

Now what? If he were seventeen he would join the army! He drove toward Hillsboro, seven miles down the highway, letting *Gooney* out until she hit sixty-five, then coasted back down to fifty. He opened the windows so the sweet night air slashed through the car.

He stopped at the outskirts of Hillsboro and bought a soft-dip ice cream cone. He drove back slowly, trying to think it through.

His big mouth had got him into real trouble this time. Why couldn't he learn to keep it shut? What would the school board do now? Suspend him for thirty days, or maybe kick him out of school for good?

A cold shiver ran down his back. Basketball! He had just faked himself out of the rest of the basketball season! Sam had won after all. The closer he came to Forestville, the more anxious he was to know what the board had decided. He stopped at the first filling station with a pay phone and called Coach Farley. The coach had just got home.

"Coach?"

"Vinny?"

"Yeah, Coach."

"Sorry, Walker."
"They expel me?"
"Yes, for the rest of the semester. That's most of the basketball season, Vinny."
"Damn!" He paused. "Thanks, Coach, for trying."
"Sure, Vinny. I don't know if I did any good or not. Guess we'll have to wait until next season."
"Yeah, thanks anyway, Coach."
"You be sure to keep in touch, Vinny, okay? And, Vinny — watch that temper."
"Okay, Coach." They hung up.
He drove home slowly. His mother was there, but she turned her head and wouldn't talk to him. She had been crying. His dad was off on a drunk somewhere. If a bar called tonight, Vinny thought, he wasn't going to drag his dad home. Let him work off his twenty-five dollar fine this time!
Vinny called Kathy. She was crying.
"What are you going to do?" She asked, sniffling.
"I don't know. Find a job, I guess."
"Doing what?"
"Busboy, boxboy, whatever I can get."
"Maybe your mother could get you on where she works."
"Hey, good idea. She might have some pull, she's been there four years."
Before they hung up Kathy made him promise to call the next day. He felt lost, cut off from school and all his friends. And no more basketball. That he was going to miss the most. He went into the living room and watched TV until 2:30 a.m.
Vinny got up at ten the next morning. He showered and dressed in a white shirt, tie, slacks and sport coat. He left the house before his mother got up, to avoid a scene, and drove to the Blue Flame where she worked. When he stopped outside he saw the sign that said it would open at 11:30 a.m. He drove back to Miller's hardware. Mr. Miller shook his head.
"Don't need any help right now, son."
Vinny tried six more stores downtown, but nobody hired him.

At noon Vinny went back to the Blue Flame. It was a restaurant-cocktail lounge. The food wasn't bad, but his mother said most people went there to drink, not eat. Vinny pushed through the door and asked for the manager. He was a small man with a heavy beard.

"Yeah, kid, whatcha want?"

"Do you need a bus boy, or kitchen help? I'm looking for a job."

"Had any experience?"

"No sir."

"Are you over eighteen?"

"No."

"Sorry, try the family restaurants where they don't serve drinks. Law ways you got to be over eighteen to work in here."

Vinny left. Eight times he'd been shot down. On the way home he stopped for a Coke at a new place called the Hamburger Haven. Vinny drank his Coke and paid for it.

"The boss around?" he asked the cashier.

"Sure is, right through that door."

Five minutes later he had a job, starting immediately. The busboy had quit two days ago and the waitresses were going crazy trying to keep up.

Vinny didn't know so many dishes existed. He did everything from clearing off the counter and tables to helping wash dishes when they were behind. He worked until ten-thirty that night. His usual shift would be from nine-thirty to six-thirty.

"Okay, Walker," said the boss, "you've got the job if you want it. Pay you two forty an hour, and you get paid every Saturday night, right?"

"Right."

"Wrong, I'm putting you down on the books at two forty cause the law says I got to. If you want the job you get two bucks an hour, take it or leave it. That's sixteen bucks a day, kid. Good money."

"I'll take it."

He had a job! Vinny drove home slowly. He parked by the house, remembering he still needed to get that spare fixed. Now he could afford it. He had a job!

Vinny ran into the house and found his dad parked in front of the TV, a beer can in his hand. Hal was still up.

"Get to bed, Hal, it's way past time," he said, ruffling Hal's hair.

Hal grinned and ran for his bedroom.

"Dumb kid, hear you got 'spelled from school," his dad said, waving an unsteady beer can. "How you ever 'spect to make a living?"

"Dad, listen to me. Will you listen?" Vinny turned off the TV and grabbed the can from his dad's hand. That got his attention.

"I got a job today, working in a restaurant. I'm making sixteen bucks a day. So you'll have to stay home and take care of Hal."

"Gimme my beer!"

"You understand, Dad? You'll have to stay home and stay sober and take care of Hal."

"Yeah, yeah, gimme my beer."

Vinny took it to the kitchen and poured it down the sink.

Shuffling steps followed him.

"What'd you do with my beer?"

Vinny pointed down the sink.

"Damned kid, who'd ya think ya are?" Larry stumbled toward Vinny and swung. Vinny reacted automatically. His left hand shot out, blocking his father's blow. His right hand was cocked but he never fired it.

"Don't ever try to hit me again, Dad." Vinny warned, trembling with anger. "And don't expect me to drag you out of any more bars. If you get drunk you can sleep off your three days in jail!"

Vinny stormed out of the room and into the bathroom. He splashed cold water onto his face. His clothes smelled like dishwater. Tomorrow he'd wear a T-shirt and suntans.

Sixteen dollars a day! His mind raced ahead, counting. He could split the grocery bill with his mother, and help pay the rent too. He should call Kathy. But it was too late.

The next morning Vinny woke at eight-thirty, dressed quickly, and drove to work, hitting the end of the breakfast rush. He swarmed into the task, clearing booths, emptying undercounter trays of dirty dishes, getting the dishwater going, hauling stacks of steaming cups and plates back to the front. It was hard work, and somebody was yelling at him all the time.

By ten-thirty the lull hit them. Vinny took a break, sitting on a bench in the kitchen. The boss came back from the bank. Vinny didn't move. The small man growled at him.

"What you doing sitting down, kid? I don't pay you to sit on your duff all day. Get moving."

"Work's all done. Marsha told me I could take a break."

"Don't back-talk me, kid! One thing I don't need around here is a loud-mouthed kid with no guts for doing the work." The boss shook his head, looking at the cook.

"How about that, Cookie? Been here almost a day and he's taking orders from looney Marsha." The small man went to Vinny and jerked him up by a fistful of T-shirt and slammed him against the walk-in freezer.

"Look, punk. You flunk out of school and think you can con me into thinking you're working. I know better, see. I can spot a goof-off like you a mile away. So shape up or get out!"

Both the cook and the boss laughed as Vinny straightened up slowly.

"Remember, kid, I don't take back-talk from some half-baked bus boy!"

Later Vinny blamed it on how tired he was. He had been working like a slave and his arms were ready to drop off. Angry blood surged in his veins at each insult.

"What did you call me?" Vinny asked, stepping up close to the little man.

"I said you're a slobby-mouthed, half-cracked bus boy. Now if you want to keep your job, get busy!"

Vinny's calm shattered in a roar of anger.

"You can take your job and shove it," he yelled. "I wouldn't work for you if I was starving."

"Then get out of here, kid, and don't come back."

Vinny threw the apron in the man's face. "You owe me for a day and a half's work."

"That's exactly what your smart mouth cost you! Now get out of here!"

He had earned that money and they had to pay him!

"You owe me for eleven hour's work, at two dollars and forty cents an hour. You pay me or I'll go to the sheriff and tell him."

"You're bluffing," the man said, sneering.

Vinny shook his head. "First I go to the sheriff where I sign a complaint, then to the labor commissioner. He'll padlock your front door."

The small man's eyes weighed him carefully, but there was a trace of fear in them.

"Okay, kid." He reached in his billfold and took out two twenties. "There, take this and don't show your face here again."

Vinny took it. "I see why you can't keep help around here," he said.

What would he do now? He had to find another job. Where? He would still have a good job if he hadn't blown his cool. Sure the guy pushed him around a little, but a quick temper had cost Vinny eighty dollars a week just like it got him kicked out of school.

He looked at the money. At least he could get his tire fixed. He headed for Joe's Shell Station.

Chapter 14

Joe Carney let Vinny fix the flat with his equipment at no charge. Vinny thanked him and drove home. He would make a sandwich and have a few glasses of milk before he went back job hunting. There *had* to be another job he could get.

His mother's car sat in the drive when he came home. Something was wrong, she should be at work. He parked in front and ran inside.

His parents sat at the kitchen table, drinking coffee.

"Sit down, Vinny," his mom said.

"Why you home, Mom? What's going on?"

"I lost my job, Vinny. I haven't said anything about it before, but we got the final news this morning. They start tearing down the Blue Flame tomorrow to make room for a luxury motel. It's a good thing you're working, Vinny, 'cause we'll need it. Of course, I got two weeks notice pay."

Vinny hated telling her what had happened to him, but he had no choice.

"Smart, kid, real smart!" his dad said.

"And I suppose you've never lost a job?" Vinny lashed back.

"Stop it, both of you. We got us a problem."

"You got a problem. I'll be seventeen in three months, then I can join the army."

"Best thing for you, give you some discipline," Larry said.

"Shut up! Both of you!" Mrs. Walker showed unaccustomed life. "In three weeks we'll be hocking stuff to buy food! I'll make some phone calls, but there are twelve other waitresses from the

Blue Flame looking for work, too."

Vinny found the weekly newspaper and looked at the classified ads. There were two ads under "boys wanted," but both were for after-school jobs. He ate a cheese sandwich and downed three glasses of milk.

"I'm going out looking for a job," he said.

No one spoke or tried to stop him. He drove downtown and began making the rounds. The manager at the Ford dealership said he would need a lot boy after the first of the year. The other hardware store, the dime stores, all four grocery stores and the lumberyard were full up.

It was three-thirty p.m. when he gave up and sat in his car thinking about it. The next job he got he wouldn't blow his cool. He'd learned the hard way. He started the car and drove past the high school. Classes were out. He parked on Jefferson half a block this side of Kathy's house.

Vinny thought about school and basketball as he waited for her. He wondered how the team would do? Vinny knew he should call the coach and talk, but somehow he couldn't. Not yet. He missed basketball more than school. A chill ran through him as he realized he might never finish high school.

He got out of the car and walked to meet Kathy. She ran toward him and threw her arms around him. He held her close.

"Vinny! Oh, I'm glad to see you!" She smiled. "It's just not the same around school without you."

"Sure, everybody's wearing black arm bands." He took her hand as they walked around the block away from her house. He told her about his one day job and how he blew it.

She squeezed his hand. "Oh, Vinny, that's a shame! But if you think you got troubles, three kids got busted on narco charges today. Took them right out of classes."

"Yeah? Tough."

"I'll say tough! Lots of things happening at school. We have one new cheer leader. Sally got pneumonia and nearly died. She's back but not leading cheers. Big game on tonight with Hillsboro. You coming?"

"Can't. School board said I can't go to any school thing."

"Darn. And the team's going to be lousy without you."

"That's what makes me so mad about getting expelled — the basketball. I lose a whole season and it never comes back."

"I know how you feel, Vinny. I was dating the star player!"

They walked farther. "I've got to go. Ever since Mom went to that hearing and you got expelled...."

"Yeah, and I can't come see you?"

"Not for a while."

"Figures."

They walked back to the car and Vinny jumped in.

"When will I see you again, Vinny?"

"When I get a job, or come back to school. Maybe even before then. I'll call, okay?" She nodded.

"Bye, Vinny."

He drove away fast, and was almost to the corner before he saw the paper on the seat. Vinny pulled to the curb and read it:

I've still got a score to settle with you. If you're man enough, meet me in the park by the drinking fountain. I'll be alone.

It wasn't signed, but Vinny knew who left it. Sam must have seen his car parked there and left the note when Vinny walked Kathy home.

He read it again. Why bother with Sam? That was all over now. But it bugged him. It would feel good to smash his fist into Sam's nose!

He gunned the Ford toward Rogers Park, knowing the spot Sam meant. It had a screen of brush almost all the way around it.

Vinny parked down the block and approached cautiously. He couldn't see anyone around the fountain. He checked again.

Sam was sitting near the far edge of the lawn. He looked around, then stretched out again. Vinny saw no one else. He circled the area and came up behind Sam. He moved cautiously, stepping out six feet from the big guy, who still hadn't heard him.

"Hi, Sam."

White jumped and sat up.

"Slipping, Sam? No lead pipe, you're not even high on speed, and you don't have your goon squad? How do you expect to win?"

Sam wasn't in a talking mood. He sprang up and slid out of his sweater. He moved toward Vinny, a sneer on his face.

Vinny had no fight plan. Sam was bigger, stronger and heavier, but Vinny knew he was in better shape. Run him to death, Vinny thought. Box him, jab him, stay away from him and run the big goon to death.

Sam came at him but Vinny danced away. Sam came in again and Vinny started back, then reversed himself and jabbed his right fist into Sam's nose, then he moved back again, keeping out of reach of the big arms.

Vinny circled, jumped, moved, kept the bigger boy in motion. He saw an opening and drove in, faking his left to the face and pounding his right into Sam's belly. Sam retaliated with a jab to Vinny's chin but it had no power.

The feinting and jabbing continued.

"Stand still and fight, yellowbelly."

Vinny laughed and jabbed Sam's jaw, stepping back again.

Sam changed his tactics and rushed, trying to grapple with Vinny, to bring him to the ground. Vinny darted to one side and all Sam caught was a handful of T-shirt. Vinny's fist slammed down hard on his wrist and Sam let go, stumbling away.

Sam was getting tired. Vinny felt like it was still the first quarter. All of the basketball passing and dribbling had strengthened his arms. He timed Sam's next rush perfectly, side-stepping it and smashing his fist against Sam's broad neck as he roared past. This time Vinny followed Sam who had lowered his arms. As he turned Vinny blasted a solid right into his chin and a left against the side of Sam's head.

Sam tried to put up his hands, but Vinny rammed a left into his mid-section and before he could move slapped his right against Sam's soft nose.

The big one bellowed in pain. He came clawing at Vinny, not boxing, but stalking an enemy runner. Vinny knew if Sam ever got his arms around him, it would be another kind of a fight.

Footwork helped Vinny stay out of reach, but now he was

backing up. He tried to watch the ground behind him, and twice circled to get back in the flat, cleared area.

They had been going at each other for ten minutes. Sam was wheezing and gulping down air. Vinny breathed hard, his arms were tired now, but not his legs.

He had to outthink the big ape. He knew Sam would charge again, and just before he did Sam always dropped his guard and hunched his shoulders. For a split second Sam was wide open. Vinny checked the ground behind them, saw Sam start to lower his arms. Vinny lashed out, his left connected with Sam's head, turning it to the right. It set up his jaw perfectly for a right which crashed against it a fraction of a second later.

Sam never got his arms up. Vinny dug his left into Sam's midsection and his right against the drooping chin.

Sam's eyes rolled, his hands fell to his sides and his knees buckled. He sat down. He wasn't unconcious but he couldn't get up. Vinny put his toe on Sam's shoulder as Sam had done to him, and pushed. He fell forward, his face skidding in the dirt, his eyes closed.

Vinny walked into the brush, shoving his T-shirt into his pants. He let his arms hang loose, breathing deeply. He heard the car before it came into sight. The cops were supposed to swing through the one road in the park every hour. He saw the white sedan through the brush.

The car drove past a gap in the shrubbery and Vinny knew it wasn't Dutch driving. Dutch never wore his helmet when he was cruising. It had to be the new cop, Harry. As the car pulled around the brush Vinny walked away from it toward the street. He had a perfect cover, good screening so Harry couldn't see him. Vinny heard the car stop and a door slam. By that time Vinny was on the sidewalk at the corner, crossing the street. If he could get to his Ford before Harry spotted him, he would be in the clear.

Chapter 15

Vinny kept walking. He hadn't left his car beside the park, but one block over. That gave him an edge. Every instant he expected the new cop to yell at him, but he didn't.

He slid into his Ford with a deep sigh of relief. Five minutes later he was home.

Vinny parked in front of the house and looked at it. It looked terribly run down. Why should he think about that now, just after he whipped Sam?

The house needed a new coat of paint. One corner sagged where one of the support beams had slipped. The yard was a mess. The tree in the skimpy lawn needed trimming. They rented the house, but they didn't take care of it.

The houses around theirs were much better. Why hadn't he noticed it before?

Inside the living room the plastered walls were dirty. The whole house was a disaster. His dad was watching TV, while Hal pretended to be doing his homework.

"Hal, better do that in the kitchen."

"I don't have to. Dad said I could do it here."

"Come on, little buddy. I used to try the same thing. Better finish it on the kitchen table."

Hal picked up his books, grumbling, but went into the other room and closed the door.

Vinny looked at the room as a visitor might. Beige linoleum on the floor in pock-marked, nine-inch squares. Beige painted walls and ceiling. One overstuffed sofa with more cigarette burns than you could count. It was all *his* fault, Vinny thought, glaring at the back of his father's head. But a showdown would have to wait. His hands were hurting now, and he was exhausted.

In the bathroom he filled the sink with cold water and let his hands soak. His right was the worst. He took two aspirins and had a shower.

At five-thirty his mother came home. She hadn't found a job either. Dinner that night was a silent affair. When they finished eating, his mother pushed back the dishes and wrote some figures on a piece of paper.

"We got forty dollars cash, that's all. The rent's due. We can put off Mr. Joerden for a while, but we got to eat."

Vinny walked around the table and put his hand on her shoulder. "I'll have a job by tomorrow, Mom. If not then, the next day. I got some friends to talk to. Maybe I could work on a dairy farm."

"Farmers don't hire in the winter, kid. You should know that," his father said.

Vinny glared. "Don't worry, Mom, we'll come up with something."

"Hell, yes, listen to the big man. He's a big stud all of a sudden." Vinny's dad stood, waving his beer can at the boy. "You got lots of growing up to do, kid."

Vinny slapped the can out of his father's hand.

"So have you, you lousy drunk! You make your wife support your family. You're not even a man!"

Larry's attitude changed. His shoulders sagged and his voice whined. "You know I'm a sick man, Vinny. Why you yelling at your daddy that way?"

Vinny doubled up his fists, but rammed them into his pockets, almost ripping the seams.

"If you're sick, it's sick in the head. Why don't you get a job and let Mom stay home for a change?" He fled from the room before he got in a brawl with his dad.

He slipped under *Gooney's* wheel and drove away before his

mother could stop him. In the next block he swerved sharply to miss an old man crossing the street. It was dark now, and his headlights hadn't picked him up until the last second. He pulled the Ford to the curb, shaking so hard he could barely hold the wheel. He'd nearly killed that old man! He turned the engine off and sat there in the dark, fighting with himself, trying to calm his jangled nerves.

At last he knew what he would do. He started the car and drove slowly to Joe Carney's Shell, using the pay phone at the corner of the lot.

"Kathy?"

"Hi, what's up?"

"Too much. Could I come over and see you? Or could you tell your mom you're going to visit a girl friend for a couple of hours. I got to talk to somebody."

"Sure, Vinny, I can pull a deal and get out. But what's the panic?"

"I just want to talk to you."

"Okay, Vinny. I'll tell Mom I'm going to the game. The JV game starts at six-thirty, remember? So I'll leave here and meet you on Jefferson Street at six-fifteen. We can talk and I can still get to the varsity game."

"Right, see you soon." He hung up and looked at the clock in the station.

Ten minutes later Vinny met her a block from school.

He caught her shoulders and kissed her. Before she could say anything he took her hand and led her down Plum Street away from school. *Gooney* was parked there. He opened the door for her and ran around to get in his side. He pushed across the seat close to her and put his arm around her shoulders.

"Kathy, what am I going to do?" He told her about the latest hassle at home. She held his hand as they talked.

"Sometimes I get so mad at my old man I think I might hurt him. He won't go out and get a job. If somebody gives him one, he's too stupid or drunk to hold it."

"Vinny, could we drive someplace? I keep thinking I see Mom

walking by."

He drove, and talked, pouring it all out. About the worry and frustration, about not having enough money, about how his dad was such a nothing, about how it really felt to get kicked out of school.

"And all this just because you get mad fast. You could prevent most of your trouble if you learned to cool it, Vinny."

"So now you're a shrink or something!" He said it fast, as his anger rose. But he tried to laugh, to show her he really didn't mean it.

He drove down Stringtown Road, crossed the tracks into a farm lane that ended behind a spattering of willows and alders near Merry Brook.

He killed the motor and the lights and put his arms around her.

"Kathy, nothing I've done in a week has turned out right. I need a good ear to listen to me, and a pretty girl to kiss me." She lifted her face to his and he kissed her hard.

"Oh, Kathy, I've got to find a job, and fast. I don't have a single good idea!"

Her head nestled against his shoulder.

"Vinny, when I think what they've done to you, I just want to cry, it makes me so mad!"

"I could be playing basketball tonight, first string!"

"That really bugs me!"

He kissed her again, long and sweet. When he finally lifted his head, Kathy pushed him away.

"Party's over Vinny. Time I got back to the game."

"Can't we stay a little longer?"

"Maybe next time. I've got to show up at that game."

"Sure, Kathy, go ahead," Vinny said, filled with self-pity. "You put me down too. Why not make it one hundred per cent?"

She laughed. "Vinny, sometimes you're simple as a little kid. I mean, I like you and all that, but not this 'car in the lane' scene. Let's go back to the bright lights."

Vinny started the car and turned around. What had suddenly brought that on? He rammed the Ford backwards, slammed on the brakes, and roared out of the bumpy lane to Stringtown Road. He drove too fast, but he didn't care. What had he done to Kathy? He was almost to the school before he could trust his voice.

"Kathy, I guess I was out of line back there," he said, not believing what he said.

"Don't sweat it, Vinny." She reached over and kissed him on the cheek.

He pulled to a stop half a block from the gym.

"No hard feelings? Give me a call soon. I've really got to get inside. Mom will check with some other kids to be sure I went to the game."

Vinny nodded. "Can I see you again?"

"Sure! Call me after school. I'll try to get the phone first." She reached for the door handle. "Vinny, would you like to kiss me again?"

He did, holding it until she pulled away. She slid out of the car in one supple movement and ran into the gym.

It was still early, so he drove to Joe's for a dollar's worth of gas. As the money drawer opened in the little office, he couldn't help but notice the stack of fives and tens. He was surprised how much money Joe had in the till by the end of the day.

He drove downtown to the Tip-Top Ice Cream Parlor. It was the main hangout for the kids, and after a game it was swamped. It would be bedlam in another hour.

Vinny had a Coke at the counter and read through the want ad section of the city newspaper. It would be a twenty mile drive each way every day, but if he could find a good job.... three columns of help wanted, male, but he found nothing that looked any good. You had to have money to invest, or be over twenty-one, or have had lots of sales experience. There were lots of jobs for carpenters and mechanics.

Vinny stared at the mechanic ad. The filling stations. He could try for a job at the stations! One of them always needed an extra man. He could fill in easy. He tried to think how many stations there were in town. Twenty, maybe twenty-five. He could start on them in the morning. He should have a job by noon! Vinny splurged and ordered a pineapple sundae. Before long the first kids from the game whooped through the Tip-Top doors.

Chapter 16

The kids suddenly seemed young to him. They didn't know how cold the outside world could be. Vinny watched them flood in. He sat at the counter against the wall watching them.

A few guys waved, one or two came over and said hi, but it wasn't the same. It felt weird. He was the same age as these kids, yet he didn't feel like one of them, and all because of Sam. Vinny waited for the anger to rise in him but it didn't. He wondered about that. Sam White, Sam White! Somehow the name or image didn't gall him the way it should.

He looked at his knuckles, which were still raw. Some of the basketball players came in, he could tell by the cheer. He didn't even look up.

Someone crowded onto the stool beside him.

"Bad scene, guy, I guess you heard we got clobbered!"

Vinny looked up at Lars Larson who held out his hand. They shook.

"They won?"

"Barely. Edged us 84 to 45. We're not a team, just five ball hogs."

"You starting at guard now?"

Lars nodded.

"Good."

Lars spun off the stool. "I got to cut out, got a bird back there."

"Play it cool," Vinny said watching Lars work his way through the packed room. Jim Hawthorne burrowed his way through the pack and slid into place beside Vinny.

"How are the wheels, man?"

Vinny thumped him on the shoulder. "Still spinning. How's the Deuce?"

"Groovy. Hear you're working."

"Working at trying to find a job."

They talked for half an hour about cars and work and school, but Vinny didn't feel right. He just didn't belong. He was "out" and they were "in." It was a bad scene all the way. He told Jim he had to cut out, and left. He'd have to be out early, ready to go look for a job.

Vinny coasted up to the house with the motor off. One light burned inside. He listened to his radio for fifteen minutes, then the last light snapped out and he went in quietly and crawled into bed.

By noon he had canvassed seven filling stations. One place needed a man, but he had to have a high school diploma. Vinny waited almost an hour at two more spots for the managers to come in. He had a list of the places he had tried. Vinny checked off another one and bought a hamburger and Coke for lunch.

That afternoon he went to six more stations. Each place he got the same business. He told them he was good on cars, could do tune-up work, minor repairs and fix flats.

"You out of high school yet, kid?" one station manager asked him. Vinny shook his head. "Kid, go back and get that diploma. Might not seem important now, but look at me, I didn't, and this is all I got."

Vinny mumbled that he was going back next semester and hurried to his Ford. He was beat. Whoever said it was easy to find a job was nuts! He parked in front of the house and checked his gas. He had a quarter of a tank. If he didn't get a job soon he'd be walking.

Inside, Vinny found his dad sleeping on the sofa and Hal watching TV. Thank goodness for the mechanical baby sitter. He slipped into his tennis shoes, shorts and sweatshirt and took off around the block. He was tired, but not muscle tired. He was up-tight from nerves and tensions as the TV commercials put it.

He ran two miles, no sprints, just a good five-minute-mile pace. When he got home he was puffing. After a shower he would feel better.

His mother was home when he came out of his bedroom. She smiled at him, and Vinny could see the worry-tension lines cutting deeper into her face.

"A big zero for me again today, Mom."

She motioned him into the kitchen where she sat on a stool peeling potatoes.

"I've got a *maybe* job in a restaurant. Nothing fancy and they don't serve drinks, so the tips won't be so good." She rubbed her forehead. "But right now a job is a job. The man said to come back tomorrow afternoon when he won't be so busy."

Vinny watched her with the knife, working over the potatoes. She was great. What she had to put up with the past fifteen years would turn a saint into a sinner.

"Mom, I'm sorry I been giving you such a bad time. The fights and arguing. But Dad seems to bug me more all the time."

She almost spoke, then stopped.

"I'm trying, Mom. These last few days have been rough, and they've pounded something into my skull. I've got to hold down my temper."

He dug into his billfold and took out twenty dollars.

"This was my pay down at that eat joint before I quit. Maybe you can put it on the rent."

Gloria Walker looked at the bill. "But Vinny, you earned it, you keep it." She said it but she couldn't stop looking at the money.

"No, Mom. You take it and use it how you want. About time I started to pay for my room and board."

She took the money and put it in her purse.

"Mom, I just hope you don't ...."

She looked up and nodded. "Vinny, I know what you mean, about not giving any to your father. But if he doesn't get anything to drink here, he'll go downtown and mooch drinks and get in trouble. That always costs more in the long run."

"Yeah, Mom, I guess it does."

"Vinny, ever think about your guitar anymore? We talked about selling it a couple of months back."

The guitar cost him forty-nine dollars two summers before. He had run a paper route and mowed lawns and saved every dime to get that electric box. Now, he never played it.

"Try them at Broderson's Music. They said they would buy it back if I got tired of it. Should be worth a few bucks."

She leaned over and touched his arm. "Vinny, I know how you worked for that guitar. I'll pay you back."

"Sure, Mom," he said grinning.

She laughed. "My little boy is growing up. He's starting to think about how other people feel."

He slept until almost noon Sunday, then took a run around the block and caught a football game on TV. In the afternoon he had a phone call from a woman asking him if he could rake leaves. He told her he would be there Monday morning.

Monday he worked hard for six hours, getting the leaves raked, and burned. When he was done the woman gave him four dollars. That would buy him gas for another month!

His mother's job fell through so she was back looking. Vinny went to several more stations Tuesday, but with no luck. He had made up his mind not to go to Joe Carney's Shell Station. Joe was such a great guy he might make a job for him, and Vinny didn't want charity. If he couldn't do any good at the last three stations on his list Wednesday, he'd have to go back to the bus boy list. There were five more restaurants in town he could try.

Vinny got home at four-thirty, tired and feeling mean. He ran again and it relaxed him, working the poison juices out through his pores instead of his fists. After his shower he called Kathy.

"Where have you been? Why haven't you called? What's going on?" she fired the questions at him like a machine gun.

"I know there are twenty-three filling stations that don't need any help."

"I'm sorry, Vinny. Hey, hear about the practice game? We lost by only four points, so we're getting better."

"Yeah, great."

"Tired?" she asked.

"Right. This job hunting isn't what I expected. It's crazy being out of school and looking for a job. It's crazy like tough and mean and hard. I've never smiled so much in my life, trying to look keen and eager. I thought it would be a cinch to get a job. Ha! So, what's new with you?"

"Wow! Not much compared with that! I mean, we've just been doing the same, dull old classes and things. There's a tryout for a junior varsity cheer leader squad and me and a couple of other girls are going to work up a team. Should be fun. But you wouldn't be interested in that."

There was a pause.

"Hear that new motel out where the Blue Flame used to be will be hiring sixty people soon as it's up and going," Vinny said. "That will be a lot of new jobs. I'm hoping I can get on there."

"Oh, the new motel? Yeah, I heard something about it." She waited a moment. "You hear about Mr. Holbeck, the shop teacher, getting a speeding ticket? He's going to fight it. Claims his speedometer is right and the cop's is wrong."

There was another pause.

"How's the team looking?"

"We haven't won one yet. Lars says there might be hope, but he's discouraged."

"See much of Lars?"

"Oh, no, once a while in the hall. He asked about you last time."

The pauses were growing longer. There wasn't anything else to say.

"I think my mother wants to use the phone," Kathy said. "But call me again."

"Right, 'bye."

He cradled the phone. Oh it was a great big happy life, sure it was! A month ago he thought everybody was holding him back, pushing him down, putting him off. Telling him to wait until he'd grown up. Now nobody was holding him back. He could go out and look for a job all day long. He could pretend he was grownup and didn't have to take sass from anybody. But he did. Anybody who worked for anybody else did. The whole lousy thing hurt a heck of a lot more now than when he was in school.

Chapter 17

Wednesday morning Vinny checked the last station on his list. It was a neighborhood spot off the main highway but on a well-traveled street.

A man in his sixties ran it. He pushed a baseball cap back on his head and scratched his thinning hair.

"Don't rightly know, son, if I need help or not. Thinking of selling the place."

"I can do tune-up work and change tires, minor service work. And I need a job," Vinny said.

"Doc told me not to work such long hours." He pulled the Expos cap down. "Tell you what, I'll talk it over with Martha, and you stop back this afternoon."

Vinny nodded and drove off. It was a slow way for the old man to say no. Vinny had been that route before.

He took out his second list, showing six family-type restaurants and coffee shops in town and along the highway. One of them was already checked off. He drove the closest one and got a quick "no" from the owner.

Vinny growled his Ford back to the Tip-Top and went in for a Coke. He made it last as he worked through the help wanted ads in the city paper again. There was a couple of them he would try for if he lived in closer, but he'd burn up half his pay for gas.

Mrs. Dyke came to ask him if he wanted anything else, so he asked her if they needed any help.

"We sure do. Our swamper got drunk last night and didn't show. Come on back."

The Tip-Top made its own ice cream, and the equipment had to be washed, the cans cleaned, the whole back of the place scrubbed down, mopped and put back together. Vinny had the job done in three hours. Mrs. Dyke smiled.

"It takes Hank all day to get that much done." She went to the cash register and brought him six dollars.

"How about tomorrow? Can I do the same job tomorrow?"

"Afraid not, Vinny. Hank never goes on a drunk for more than one day at a time. If he does he gets fired and he needs the job."

Vinny picked up his jacket and walked out. You do a good job, better than the regular man, and still they won't hire you. He kicked at the curb. At least he had the six dollars.

Dinner that night went okay. Vinny was determined to get along with his dad. His mother had looked all day and found nothing. His dad was not drunk for a change. Vinny held his tongue and tried not to make him angry. It worked. After dinner he drove over to see Kathy. He figured her mother would at least let him in the house by now.

Kathy opened the door when he rang.

"Hey, gee! Come on in. I was just thinking about you."

He went inside and she waved at her homework.

"What do you need help on?"

"Algebra!" She moaned. "It's absolutely the most fantastically complicated stuff I've ever seen."

Vinny looked at the problems.

"Nothing to it. Just work the factors inside the parens first, then carry it out. Here." He did one problem for her.

"Is that all there is to it?"

"That's all." Vinny turned to see Mrs. Bell watching.

"Oh, it's you. Vinny, isn't it? I hope you're not going to disturb Katherine while she's doing her homework."

"Oh, Mother! Vinny just solved my big hang-up on algebra. I asked you to help me, remember, but you didn't know how."

Mrs. Bell frowned and went into the next room.

"Sometimes she makes me furious!" Kathy said, scowling. She shrugged. "How goes the battle?"

"Better."

"Get mad at anyone today?"

"You kidding? Of course."

"What happened?"

He told her about the Tip-Top job.

"Sure you did it right?"

"Yes, it was a snap. I could do that job standing on my head, yet they let this other guy keep it. I step in and do the work, and twice as fast as the regular guy, but do I get the job? No!"

"You did do a good job?"

"Sure, Mrs. Dyke said so. And I worked fast and hard. If he gets two bucks an hour for that job, he better not get drunk very often or I'll have it."

"Did you enjoy the work?"

"Enjoy?" He had to think. "No, it was wet and dirty, and the smell of that sour milk, Wow! I sure wouldn't want to do that kind of work all the time."

"You really don't sound too mad about it, now."

He considered that. "Well, I guess I'm not, but two bucks an hour, that still sounds great!"

He closed her algebra book. "How about asking your mom if we can go up to the Tip-Top for a sundae? We can walk, tell her."

"Well, I'll ask."

She came back a few moments later.

"No, you can't go out. You have your homework to do," Kathy said mimicking her mother's voice.

Vinny laughed. "You should be on the stage."

Kathy didn't think it was funny. He leaned close to her. "Meet you same place Friday night for a drive before the game?"

She nodded, "But not to Stringtown Road."

"I'd better get out of here."

They walked to the door and Kathy stepped outside and kissed him quickly. She leaned back before her mother could see her.

"I'll pick you up on Jefferson on Friday, right?"

"Right. Sorry about tonight. Sometimes the Ancient One can be very dull."

"I wouldn't get mad if you said that again."

She waved as he ran out and jumped into *Gooney*. He drove to Sunset Highway, the main road through town, and parked below the Chevron station across from the Tip-Tip. He watched the people and the cars, because he didn't want to go home.

A few minutes later he decided to go have a Coke at the Tip-Top. He had to break a bill to pay for it, but he had seven dollars left. He would give most of that to his mom to help buy the food. Vinny felt terribly alone, sitting there with his drink. Nobody else was around, the place was dead. He drained the last bit of ice from his glass and headed back for *Gooney*.

Before he started the engine he checked the gauges. He hadn't been watching closely enough and was down past a quarter of a tank. He liked to keep it as full as he could to prevent water condensation in the tank, but he didn't want to drive the mile back to Joe's station. Feeling a little disloyal, he wheeled in to the Standard pumps.

"Give me a buck's worth," he said reaching for his wallet.

It wasn't there! Vinny checked the other pocket, then his shirt pocket. "Hold it on the gas," he told the attendant.

He got out of the car and searched beneath the seat. It wasn't there, either.

A cold sweat beaded his forehead. Seven bucks! Where was his billfold? Lost? It couldn't be! In the Tip-Top? He remembered taking it out to pay for his Coke, but did he ever put it back? Did he leave it on the counter?

He waved at the attendant, drove out and parked outside the Tip-Top. He looked where he had been sitting. His glass was still there, but no billfold. He asked the waitress if she had seen a billfold on the counter. She shook her head, and hurried away to take an order. Nothing had been turned in at the cashier's counter.

Seven dollars! Seven hard-earned dollars. How could he have been so stupid? A new thought hit him. Maybe he had dropped it at Kathy's. No, he had it here, and had taken a dollar bill from it to buy the Coke.

Or did he? Maybe he *had* dropped it or it slipped out of his pocket at Kathy's house. He really didn't believe it, but there was the faintest chance, and he had nothing to lose by checking.

He ran to *Gooney* and jumped in. It was only a few blocks. A car was parked in front of her house. He drove slowly towards it, and when a door opened he parked at the curb and turned out his lights. Two persons got out. One looked like Kathy! He started his motor and edged up slowly toward them, pulling into the middle of the street to pass the car in front of her house. Just as he did, the porch light snapped on at the Bell house, revealing Kathy and Lars Larson kissing. Mrs. Bell opened the door and they flew apart.

Vinny drove on past, his mind churning. Lars and Kathy? When did it all happen? He and Kathy weren't going steady, but after the other night...?

He parked down the block. He couldn't go to the basketball games, but Lars could. And Lars was a big varsity starter. Kathy really wanted a basketball player boyfriend like Jim said. He should have listened to Jim.

He slammed his hand down on the steering wheel. That sneaky little broad! Dating two guys at once.

If he had a better car ... sure and how could he get a better car? He couldn't even hold onto seven dollars. His driver's licence was gone too! It would cost him three dollars to get a duplicate. Money! Why did everything hinge on money?

If he or his mom didn't get a job soon, they'd have to go on welfare just to eat. The money was all but gone. The rent was past due and the grocery shelf at home was almost bare. At least his old man couldn't bum from his mom to go on any more three-day drunks.

Money! The world revolved around money! It came back to the filthy-green every time. If you had it you could solve a lot of your problems.

How did a guy get money? A job? Sure, but where?

Borrow? Sure, from whom? The picture of that cash drawer at

Joe's Shell and the stack of fives and tens kept coming into his mind. There must have been two or three hundred dollars in there.

He wouldn't even think about anything like that! Joe was one of his best friends. Joe Carney had loaned him tools when he needed them. Joe had given him five gallons of gas on credit once until he got paid for a leaf-raking job. Who else in town would do that? Joe had even given his dad a job, knowing that he wasn't going to last.

It was ridiculous even considering getting money from that cash drawer.

Vinny drove slowly up Sunset Highway, turning a block before he came to Joe's Shell Station. He went up the far side of the block and came back where he could watch the office from half a block away.

Joe wasn't working; his night man was on, some new guy Vinny didn't know. If he didn't know the attendant, neither would this guy know him!

There were no customers. The man sat in the office where the cash box was. It wasn't a cash register, just a drawer in the desk. No bell to ring, no key. Vinny shivered. It would settle the money problem for a while. He drove to the end of the block and pointed his car away from the station, leaving it at the end of the alley.

He went up the alley at a half trot. It opened just behind the station. As soon as a car came in for gas he would sprint to the back of the station building, and slip into the lube area. If the guy came back he would hide in the oil room. When he had a chance he would dart around the door into the office, open the drawer, take out the bills and close it. It would be like swiping candy from the dime store!

Everything went as Vinny had planned. He had just lifted the bills from the drawer when another car drove into the station. It was Joe Carney! Furiously Vinny stuffed the bills back in the drawer and ran past the lube rack and up the alley.

A sweat broke out on his forehead as he pounded up the alley. There was no one behind him. Had Joe seen his face? Could he identify him to the police? How soon would they come for him?

Should he get in his Ford and keep running? Dumb, Vinny told himself. Dumb. If they wanted him they could put out a radio alarm and pick him up anytime.

Vinny slammed the door on *Gooney* and started the car. He knew it was useless to run, but that didn't make any difference. He knew he was driving too fast, and it was crazy, because he didn't have the slightest idea where he was going.

Chapter 18

He turned onto the highway below town and drove carefully, staying within the speed limit, forty-five, then at fifty-five, and at last at sixty-five on the open road. He felt a high-speed miss in the engine as the voltage thinned out, and dropped back to fifty, humming along the two-lane highway, twisting into the hills in back of Forestville.

He drove for ten minutes, letting the fear, the frustration, the shame sweep over him time and time again.

Why had he done such a stupid thing? Why? He had no answer.

Vinny turned around at a wide spot where the trucks sometimes stopped on the long crawl up the grade. He drove back more slowly. He opened the windows and let the cold, night air blast through the Ford.

No longer did he ask "why?" He knew he would never have an answer, not for himself, not for Joe Carney, not for the police. The flight and fright and revulsion were over, washed away in the clean night air.

He expected to be picked up as soon as he came into the city limits. He drove well under the speed limit, but he saw no police cars as he drove through town to Tenth Street. He couldn't make himself drive past Joe's station, even though he could see no police cars there.

Vinny parked in front of his house. No strange cars were in sight. He sat a moment, breathing deeply. It might be hardest waiting for them to come. Why didn't they come now?

He got out and went to the front porch. A man sitting there spoke before Vinny saw him.

"Hello, Vinny."

It was Joe Carney. Vinny's heart sank.

"I been waiting for you, Vinny. Hoped you'd stop by the station. I heard you been asking for a job at the other stations around town, so I guessed you'd see me too."

Vinny sat down on the steps beside the man. He didn't know what to think. Was this some kind of trap? No, not Joe, he wouldn't trap anyone.

"I need somebody to open for me. Supposed to open by six, mornings, but lately I ain't been getting down there until seven or after. Losing lots of business from guys going to work."

Joe's eyes, even in the dim light of the street lamp, were bright, anxious.

"You *do* want a job?"

"Yeah, Joe." He paused. "But I decided not to come to your station."

"Why? I try to be good to you."

"Too good, Joe. After what Dad did to you, I figured the Walkers had done you enough harm. I don't want you feeling sorry for us."

"Vinny, I ain't a charity outfit. You don't pay your keep, I'll bounce you quick as the next guy."

He stood up. "Getting late. Six o'clock comes early. Wouldn't want you late first day."

He handed a key ring to Vinny. "I'll be there in the morning to show you how to open up, where the lights are, the pump locks and the cash drawer. Now don't be late, cause I figure on being back in bed by six-fifteen."

Vinny handed back the keys. "I can't do it, Joe. I can't work for you."

"Why not?"

"You know!"

"I need a good man at the station. You can do the job. You need the work. What else is there to know?"

"Didn't you see me at the station tonight?"

Joe didn't reply.

"I was there, Joe. You saw me. I was trying to steal money from your cash drawer."

"Like I said, Vinny, it's getting late. I want you on time in the morning."

"I tried to steal from you, Joe. You could have me put in jail. Don't you care?"

Joe grabbed Vinny by both shoulders. His hands gripped tightly.

"Of course I care, Vinny! That's why I'm not yelling cop. That's why I came here tonight to get you working for me instead of waiting until tomorrow."

Vinny shook his head. "Joe, I tried to steal from you. How can you trust me now?"

Something in Joe's eyes stopped Vinny. Joe's voice was low when he spoke.

"Long time ago, Vinny, when I was sixteen, I got into some trouble in another state. Six months in a county jail, it cost me. It took me five years to get over it." Joe let go of his shoulders.

"Six, tomorrow morning," he said and walked down the sidewalk and across the street.

Vinny watched him until he was out of sight, then went into the house and got ready for bed.

His alarm went off at five-thirty. Vinny scrambled out of bed, dressed and grabbed a quick breakfast. He was waiting at the station when Joe Carney drove in.

Fifteen minutes later Vinny had on an official Shell uniform shirt and understood how things worked. Everything was unlocked and ready to go.

Not a word was said about the previous night.

"I'll be back about ten o'clock. Any questions?"

Vinny shook his head.

"You can only work eight hours, so you'll get an hour for lunch and work until three o'clock.

A customer drove in. Vinny filled the car with gas, wiped the windshield and made change. The man was in a rush.

"One question you haven't asked, Vinny. About how much you're making?"

"Joe, I don't think I could take any money from you for a long time."

"That'll get me in troubled with the labor commissioner and juvenile court. You're making three dollars an hour. Now quit worrying."

Joe gunned his pickup and roared out of the station. Vinny pumped three hundred and forty gallons of gas before Joe came back. He nodded at Vinny's report.

"Aren't you going to check it against the cash box?"

"No."

"But after last night, I thought...."

"Vinny, quit punishing yourself. Drop it! Nothing happened last night, understand? Nothing. Wipe it off the books. Forget it." When Vinny nodded, Joe grinned.

"We've got a tune-up on that Chevy and two tires to fix before noon. Which one do you want?" Vinny tore into the tire jobs, plugging small nail holes in tubeless casings.

He couldn't believe time was moving so quickly. At eleven o'clock Vinny went for a take-out hamburger from the stand down the street. He ate and worked.

At one-thirty the night man, E.J. Brown, came on. Vinny worked the second island when more than one car was in at a time. Usually E.J. was on the pump and Vinny washed the windshield and glass all around the car. E.J. checked under the hood and the customer was rolling before he knew he had stopped.

At three-thirty Joe chased Vinny out, after giving him two pairs of tan pants and another Shell shirt. He checked to be sure Vinny still had his keys, then waved him off.

At home, Vinny found his mother crying. His father lay stretched out on the floor, a burning cigarette eating a hole in the linoleum tile. Vinny put it out and sat down beside his mother.

"Vinny, what you been doing?"

"I'm working, Mom. Got a job down at Joe Carney's Shell Station. Joe hired me at three dollars an hour, eight hours a day."

"Oh, Vinny. I knew something good had to happen soon." She was crying again. "I kept your father off the bottle for a whole week, Vinny. Then I just couldn't stand to listen to him any more. Today I almost had a job, but I got there five minutes too late. When I got home I found him like this."

"Mom, you go lay down for a while. I want you to just stay home and keep house and rest. I'm working now. We'll get the bills paid, and I'll get dinner tonight."

He stared at his dad, finally picking him up and carrying him to the sofa. After pulling off his shoes, Vinny covered him with a blanket.

He turned to the kitchen, checking the food supply. It was still early for dinner. But he felt good. It had been a long time since he had fixed dinner.

Chapter 19

The first full week of work went past so quickly Vinny could hardly believe it. He did two tune-ups, fixed a dozen tires and did ten lube and oil change jobs. It didn't seem like work at all.

Without realizing it, Vinny began picking up little gestures and mannerisms of Joe Carney. The most obvious was a big grin and a cheerful, "Hi, how are you today?" before he asked a customer what he wanted.

One rainy day they had every job done, the racks cleaned, the tire work all finished. Vinny and Joe sat in the tiny glass-walled office.

"Vinny, when the second semester starts, I'm firing you."

He looked up, but his boss wasn't joking.

"You'll be going back to school along the end of January, and Coach Farley says he has three more games after that. He's hoping you'll still want to play."

Vinny hadn't thought about going back to school. He wanted to. It just hadn't entered his mind for the past week. If Joe wanted him to go back ....

"Coach says you'll have to try out again, see if you can still play the game."

"Can I still work here, too?"

"The law says you can work and go to school eight hours a day, total. You'll be going to school five hours. That gives you three hours to work. We can figure it out. Maybe I'll give you a vacation from the start of the second semester until the end of basketball season. Then you can come back and work after that."

Vinny shaded his eyes and turned away, watching the rain. He wasn't sure if he could talk.

"Joe, I'm not very good saying thanks. I just don't know what we would have done without you."

"Yeah, okay, forget it." He stood up. "Think I forgot to close one of my pickup windows." He went into the lube rack area.

Vinny watched him go. What a guy! *What a great guy!*

It was still raining at four o'clock when Vinny drove home. His mother was in the kitchen and he could smell fresh bread.

"Hey, you haven't made homemade bread for years," Vinny yelled.

"Be done in ten minutes," she said smiling.

She looked better, Vinny thought. The rest had brought some natural color back to her cheeks. The worry lines had faded around her eyes, and she was wearing her hair differently.

"Mom, you look good enough to be one of those hostesses at some swanky spot. There are three or four down at Hillsboro."

"You really think so?"

"Sure, and who knows the business better than you?"

She looked thoughtful as he went to his room. A few minutes later he came out in his running clothes.

"You running in the rain, Vinny?"

"Sure, I won't melt. Save a big chunk of that warm bread for me." He did a one-mile circuit and came home puffing and wet to his skin. After a hot shower, he munched on the warm bread and jam.

"Where's Dad?"

"I'm not sure. He borrowed five dollars from my purse, so he's probably downtown. It's been quite a while, Vinny."

At seven-fifteen Vinny started out the front door to go cruising. The phone stopped him. He ran and picked it up.

"Hello," he said. "Sure, I've got it. Bob's Place. I'll be right down."

Vinny told his mother where he was going and ran out the front door. It was still raining.

Ten minutes later Vinny parked *Gooney* down from the bar. He turned off the engine and sat there a moment listening to the rain hit the roof.

He ran for Bob's Happy Time Bar and pushed in through the door. He waved at the barman and saw his dad in the side booth, half-way back.

"Hey, kid. Your mama know you're out?" a man at the bar called.

Vinny grinned and waved at him as he walked past to the booths.

One more time, Vinny thought. His father slumped against the wall, his head on his arms. Vomit stained his shirt sleeves. Vinny caught one hand, pulling his father to the front of the booth and lifted. He groaned and stumbled to his feet.

Vinny hardly noticed the bilish stink of vomit or the urine-stained trousers. He walked and dragged the man to the bar, resting on a stool.

"He owe you anything?" Vinny asked the barman.

"Not this time."

"You still rolling drunks, kid?" the heckler called.

"Hell, yes, Big Al. So hurry up and pass out," Vinny shot back, a big grin on his face. The rest of the crowd in the bar roared at that and Al had to buy a round.

Vinny worked his burden outside and was glad when the fresh rain washed over them.

Now if that new cop wanted to pick his Ford apart, it would be a perfect evening, Vinny thought. But he wasn't going to get mad and blow his cool.

It took several minutes to get his dad up the street to the car and stowed safely in the back seat.

Vinny sat behind the wheel, puffing. He was out of shape. He'd need to start working out hard if he wanted to run with the Forestville Vikings second semester.

He drove carefully toward Twelfth Street. Just past Eighth he heard a tire start hissing every time it went around. A flat!

He pulled to the curb and stopped. He could drive four more blocks to Joe's Shell, but that would ruin the tire.

He laughed as he got out the bumper jack and the spare. He'd change it right here in the rain. He wouldn't melt, he had just told his mother so!

FOR INTENSIVE STUDY

Chapter 1

1. How do you feel about Vinny Walker after reading chapter 1? How does the author make you feel this way?
2. Describe the setting of the story.
3. Do you think the behavior of the "rookie" officer in this chapter is typical of the police force? Why?
4. Do you mistrust policemen? Explain your answer. Do you think your answer is typical of most teenagers?
5. What do we learn about Vinny's abilities in chapter 1?
6. Explain the following: (a) heckled (b) bar rats (c) drunk tank

Chapter 2

1. Why was Vinny suspended?
2. Was his expulsion justified?
3. What new conflict is revealed to us in chapter 2?
4. Write a short paragraph describing Gloria Walker.
5. Explain: (a) unprovoked attack (b) lettermen (c) JV squad

Chapter 3

1. Write a short paragraph describing your first impressions of Kathy Bell. Refer to it at the conclusion of the story. Do you think you were correct in your assessment of Kathy?

Chapter 4

1. Mrs. Bell did not like Vinny. Why?

2. The author builds our sympathy for Vinny in this chapter. How does he accomplish it?

Chapter 5

1. What happened to Vinny's father in chapter 5?
2. Did Kathy really care about Vinny's problems? Prove your answer by referring to the story.
3. The author uses Lars as a "hired gun" in this chapter. Write a sentence to explain that statement.

Chapter 6

1. What new events complicate the plot in this chapter?
2. Are you looking forward to the events in the next few chapters? Why? How would you resolve the dispute between Sam and Vinny?

Chapter 7

1. Vinny accuses his mother, "You ain't got no time!" Do you think he was justified in talking to his mother this way? Why?
2. How does Vinny's "Revenge Caper" become serious business?

Chapter 8

1. How does Sam White get his revenge in this chapter?
2. Why do you think Vinny wants so desperately to "make the varsity team?"

Chapter 9

1. Write a short paragraph describing Coach Farley's method of coaching. Talk to your school coach and re-

port to the class on his coaching method and philosophy.

2. How does the author keep the reader's interest during this chapter, which deals mainly with the choosing and training of the school team?

Chapter 10

1. Do you think the author played high school basketball himself? Explain your answer with references to the text.
2. Sam White's pals have a surprise for Vinny in this chapter. What is it?
3. How does coach Farley show his "intestinal fortitude" in chapter 10?

Chapter 11

1. Vinny forms a new friendship in this chapter. What happens to cement that friendship?

Chapter 12

1. How does the author attempt to change our feelings about Larry Walker? Did you change your opinion about him?
2. Do you agree that Vinny had to fight Sam as a "matter of honor?"

Chapter 13

1. Do you think Vinny acted foolishly by "blasting" Mr. Green and the school board? Explain you answer.
2. Was the board justified in expelling Vinny for his outburst? Why?
3. How did Vinny lose his first job?

Chapter 14

1. Did you find chapter 14 exciting reading? What "turned you on?" Do you think Vinny has heard the last of Sam?

Chapter 15

1. What attraction does Vinny hold for Kathy?
2. Make a list of all the people who rejected Vinny and tell how they did.
3. What piece of information near the end of this chapter gives us a hint of following events?

Chapter 16

1. Why did the kids suddenly seem young to Vinny?
2. List the factors that prevented Vinny from finding a steady job.
3. Kathy and Vinny have trouble communicating in this chapter. Why do you think this happens?

Chapter 17

1. In this chapter we see the final rejection of Vinny by society. How does it come about?
2. Vinny seems to react in a predictable pattern when he is emotionally upset. What is that pattern?
3. Did you expect Vinny to steal the money from Joe Carney? Why?

Chapter 18

1. Two men had faith in Vinny. Who were they and how did they show that faith?

Chapter 19

1. What message is Chet Cunningham trying to give us in this book?
2. Did you like the ending? What do you think lies ahead for Vinny?

FOR REFERENCE AND DISCUSSION

1. What family-life patterns are depicted in the story? Are they like or unlike patterns with which you are familiar?
2. What leads Vinny and Sam to act as they do throughout the story: love? anger? hate? ambition? revenge? religion? vague impulse? loyalty? social pressure? mores? insult? honor? poverty? prejudice? ignorance? inner drive?
3. Does anyone's character change during the story? What caused the change?
4. Do a detailed character sketch of:
   (a) Vinny
   (b) Sam
   (c) Kathy
   (d) Vinny's father
5. Write a letter to Chet Cunningham and ask him pertinent questions about himself and his novel.
6. Psychologists tell us that character is shaped by two main factors: (a) heredity and (b) environment. Which factor do you think is most influential? Research this question and organize a debate on the topic. Invite a university psychologist to speak to your class on the subject. What influenced Vinny and made him the way he was?
7. Make a report on alcoholism and its effects. Should drunks be treated as criminals and thrown into the city jail? Write an essay outlining your attitudes towards alcohol.
8. Are you in favour of breathalyzer tests for drunk drivers? Make an in depth study of the machine and explain how it works to your class.
9. What types of conflict are depicted in this story: man vs. man? man vs. nature? man vs. fate? man vs. himself?

10. Do you think the people in this story behave like real people? How can you judge? When is the story realistic?
11. Write a detailed book review of this novel. Did the author succeed in communicating with young people? Have your book review published in the school newspaper.
12. Would this novel make a good film? What actors/actresses would you choose to portray the characters if you were the casting director? What movies have you seen recently that deal with a similar theme?
13. What was the general effect of the book on you? What made you feel the way you did?
14. Write a paragraph discussing the most interesting incident in the book. What made it interesting to you?
15. What broader understanding has this book given you of human nature? Do factors like love, greed, or prejudice affect the relationship among the characters?
16. Did you like this story? Would you recommend it? What age level? Why?
17. Write a poem about rejection; frustration; loneliness; ego; alcohol; violence; rivalry, etc.
18. Bring in a person on welfare or somebody who has recently lost a job to talk to the class about his/her experiences.
19. This is "contemporary novel". Explain what that means and draw up a list of other contemporary novels.
20. Take a chapter of this novel and rewrite it as a stage play or T.V. movie. Produce and present it.
21. There are some violent scenes in this novel. Do you think the use of violence is growing in our society? Why, and if so, is there an antidote?